J. R. R. Tolkien's great work of imaginative fiction, *The Lord of the Rings*, tells the story of an epic quest. The hobbit, Frodo, with the help of companions at different stages, undertakes a hazardous journey to Mordor. The narrative moves through countless changes of scene in the imaginary world of Middle-earth; a world which is totally convincing in its detail.

Journeys of Frodo is an Atlas of fifty-one maps covering that journey. It serves as a companion to the three books of *The Lord of the Rings*, to be used whilst reading (and re-reading) the story. It will help the reader to envisage the country through which the route passes and to keep track of each day's adventures.

The fifty-one maps of the book are drawn in two colours throughout, at various scales, from 100 miles to the inch to $\frac{1}{4}$ mile to the inch. Tolkien used feet and miles when measuring distances in Middle-earth. Frodo's route (together with the paths taken by other principal characters) is reproduced in red, as are the contour lines. The maps are based on clear and detailed descriptions and measurements given in the text and on the original endpaper maps. Barbara Strachey has also studied Tolkien's own beautiful drawings of the landscape and features of Middle-earth.

Each map has extensive notes to explain special points and to give references for the information used. On the rare occasions when problems of interpretation arise (and J. R. R. Tolkien was splendidly consistent) they are discussed in the relevant map's notes.

Barbara Strachey is not a cartographer or a professional artist. She has known and loved the books since they first appeared and has long wanted fuller and more detailed maps to go with them. Finally she decided to create them herself and her efforts will give the reader of *The Lord of the Rings* a new and more vivid idea of Middle-earth and the country through which Frodo and his companions passed.

JOURNEYS OF FRODO

An Atlas of
J.R.R. TOLKIEN'S
The Lord of the Rings

BARBARA STRACHEY

London
UNWIN PAPERBACKS
Boston   Sydney

First published by Unwin Paperbacks 1981
Reprinted 1984, 1985

UNWIN® PAPERBACKS
40 Museum Street, London WC1A 1LU, UK

Unwin Paperbacks
Park Lane, Hemel Hempstead, Herts HP2 4TE, UK

George Allen & Unwin Australia Pty Ltd
8 Napier Street, North Sydney, NSW 2060, Australia

ISBN 0 04 912011 5

Printed in Great Britain at the Alden Press, Oxford

FOREWORD

When I first read *The Lord of the Rings* I wished I had a complete set of maps covering the journeys of Frodo and his companions. Each time I reread the books I felt the same way, and finally I decided to compile such an atlas myself.

This is, of course, based on the very clear and detailed descriptions to be found in the text of *The Lord of the Rings*. I have also consulted *The Hobbit, Unfinished Tales* and *Pictures by J. R. R. Tolkien*, in addition to the maps in the books themselves. At times, however, I believe that the latter differ from the text or from each other in matters of spelling, distances and relationships, and in these cases I have tried to follow the written information.

The fifty maps and the Frontispiece are drawn to different scales varying from $\frac{1}{4}$ mile to the inch to 100 miles to the inch. Tolkien used feet and miles, not metric measurements, and therefore so have I. The numbers round the edges of the maps represent the distance in miles north/south and west/east of Hobbiton Hill, which is used as the 0, or 'Greenwich' point in each case. Contour lines, drawn in red, are 50, 100 or 200 feet apart according to the scale. Here and there I have added geographical details such as tributary streams, contour indications or paths and villages, which are for the most part implied but not specifically mentioned in the text. These do not, I trust, contradict, but only support existing evidence, and are, of course, not given names.

The evidence is – as one might expect – splendidly consistent. I have found only one or two difficult points which I have dealt with in the notes to the relevant maps.

I have tried to use all the topographical logic I can summon to make the maps complete, consistent at all scales and self-explanatory, but I am not a cartographer and I have deliberately not tried to work on the basis of projections, but drawn everything as though the earth were still flat and not spherical. We know, however, from *The Silmarillion* that after the Change of the World it was, in fact, spherical. No doubt this is unscientific of me, but I can only hope that the majority of those who read and enjoy the books will not worry unduly and that the minority who are experts will forgive me.

The route is marked in red, or red and black where it runs along an existing path or road.

I have marked the places where the travellers slept wherever possible, and given each day's journey its date by the Hobbit calendar, using the English names for the months. Major events are also marked. I have given references only to the chapter title and Book, as page numbers are different in the various hardback and paperback editions of both the British and American publishers and, therefore, page references would be confusing. For clarity, Book 1 refers to *The Fellowship of the Ring*, Book 2 to *The Two Towers* and Book 3 to *The Return of the King*.

I have also added symbols showing the phases of the moon. The evidence for this is based on the Full Moon noted on 8th January, the night the travellers reached Hollin (Book 1, The Ring Goes South), also confirmed by Sam on the Anduin (Book 1, The Great River). The next firm point is the New Moon which occurs on their seventh day on the River (i.e. 22nd February), while they see 'a thin crescent' the next night (Book 1, The Great River) when they are attacked by Orcs.

The next Full Moon is seen by Frodo and Sam at Henneth Annûn on 7th March. There is a slight difficulty here, as Éomer states on 6th March that the Riders would reach Dunharrow in three days, and that night (i.e. 9th March) the moon would be one day past full, thus putting the Full Moon on 8th not 7th.

The next Full Moon after this (6th April?) tallies with 'the round moon' seen at the Field of Cormallen on 8th April. Working backwards from these points and allowing a $29\frac{1}{2}$ day cycle, on the assumption that all was the same (or very nearly) as it is today, it is possible to establish all the other phases.

It should perhaps be noted that the 'Young moon' Frodo saw, when in Tom Bombadil's house he dreamt of Gandalf's escape from Orthanc, must have been the moon actually shining as he slept, a brand new crescent, and not the one Gandalf would have seen. This would have been half full and waning that night (18th September, see Book 3, Appendix B).

CONTENTS

A GUIDE TO MAP SYMBOLS

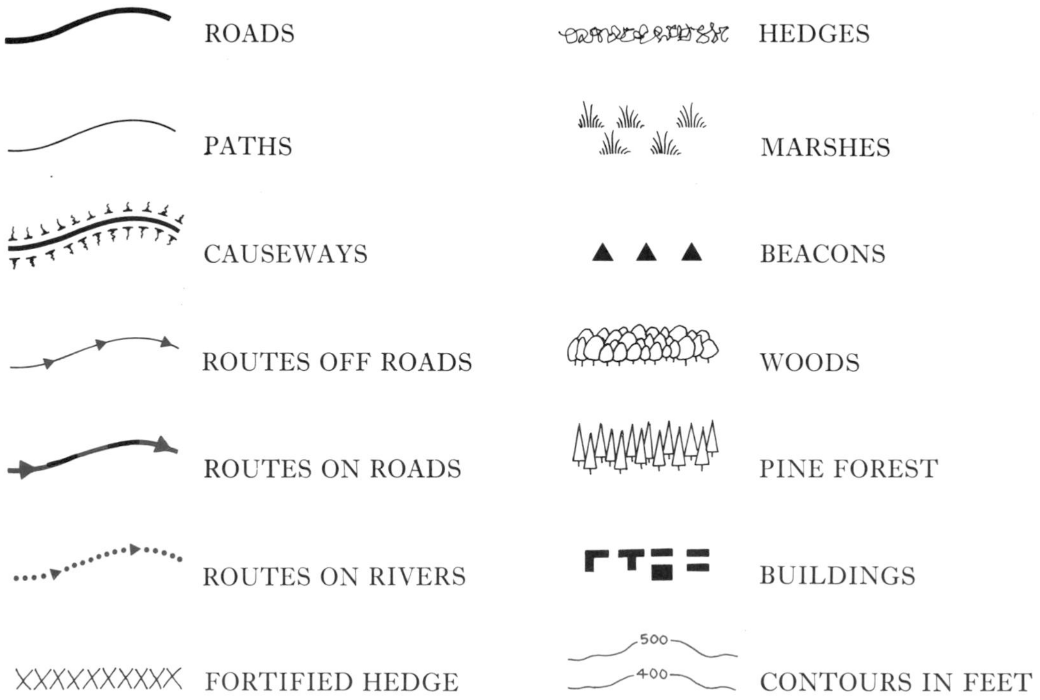

ROADS

PATHS

CAUSEWAYS

ROUTES OFF ROADS

ROUTES ON ROADS

ROUTES ON RIVERS

XXXXXXXXXX FORTIFIED HEDGE

HEDGES

MARSHES

▲ ▲ ▲ BEACONS

WOODS

PINE FOREST

BUILDINGS

CONTOURS IN FEET

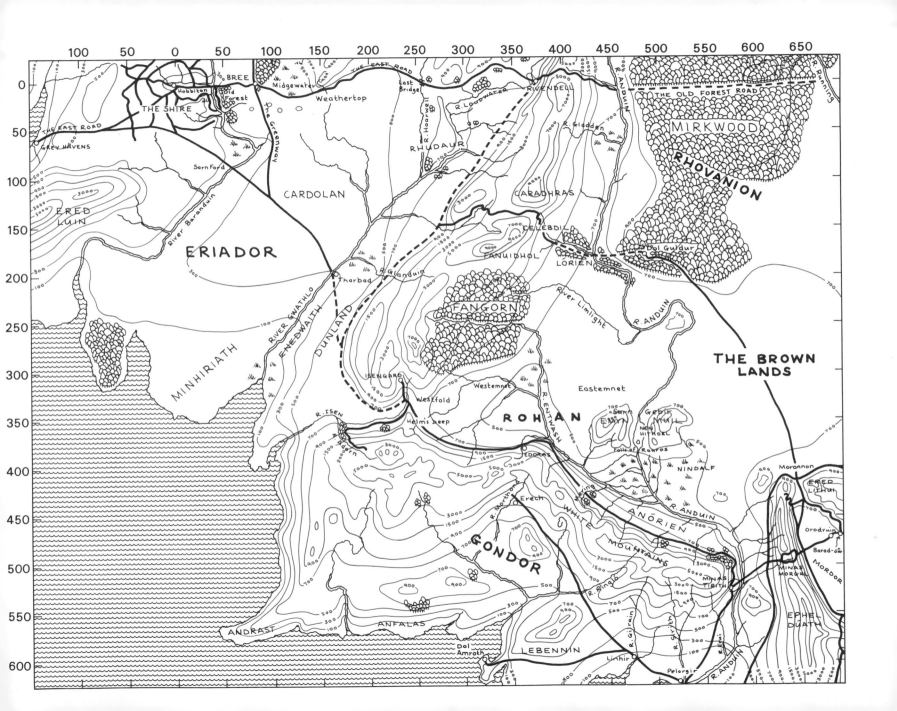

1. Hobbiton to Brandywine Bridge

This map is, of course, based on the very clear and detailed map, *A Part of the Shire*, which appears in *The Fellowship of the Ring*.

I have put Hobbiton and Bywater closer together (the Book map sets them about 4 miles apart) as in *The Hobbit* it is noted that from Hobbiton to Bywater was 'a whole mile or more' (Roast Mutton; *The Hobbit*). Bilbo did the run in 10 minutes, so if it had been four miles he would have achieved a remarkable world record – particularly in view of his short legs.

I have spelt Waymeet as it is spelt in the text (The Scouring of the Shire; Bk 3), not Waymoot, as in the map.

Frogmorton was 22 miles from the Bridge and 18 miles from Bywater, and the Three-Farthing Stone was some 4 miles east of Bywater. (The Scouring of the Shire; Bk 3.)

I have marked Causeway banks for both the roads leading into Stock. I imagine that Stock was built on a small rise above the marsh, like the city of Ely in the Cambridgeshire marshes of East Anglian England, or it would have been an unhealthy place for a village. Details of the route will be seen in Maps 3 to 5.

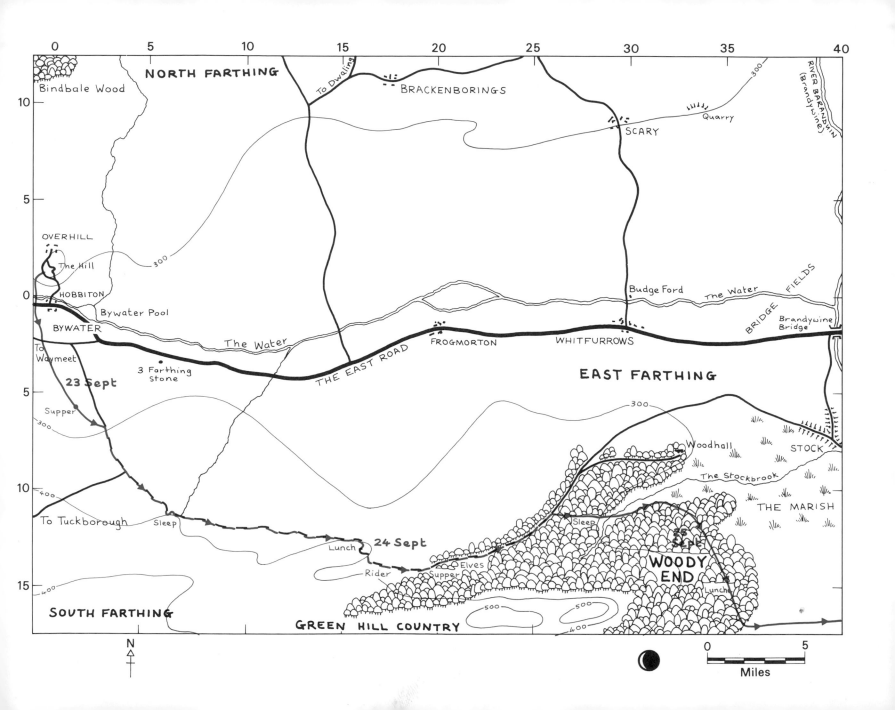

2. Hobbiton to Bywater

The map of the Hill is based on the picture in *The Hobbit*, which shows clearly that the road from Hobbiton to Overhill runs *west* of the Hill, not east, as drawn in the map *A Part of the Shire* in *The Fellowship of the Ring*.

The Gamgees lived in No 3 Bagshot Row. I imagine that the numbering would start in the east, where the Row branched off the through road.

When Bilbo overslept and had to run all the way from Bag End to Bywater, it is said that he went past the Mill and over the Water to the Inn, which we know was *The Green Dragon* and the last house on the Hobbiton side of Bywater. (The Scouring of the Shire; Bk 3.) It seems to me, however, that he would have done better to have taken a short cut across the fields. There must have been a bridge of some sort over the Water at the west end of Bywater Pool to give access to the Smials along the north shore. (The Scouring of the Shire; Bk 3.)

The map shows the avenue of trees along the road by the edge of the Pool which were cut down by the Chief's men (The Scouring of the Shire; Bk 3) and also the Old Grange (which must have been the large house west of the road in the picture) and Sandyman's Mill.

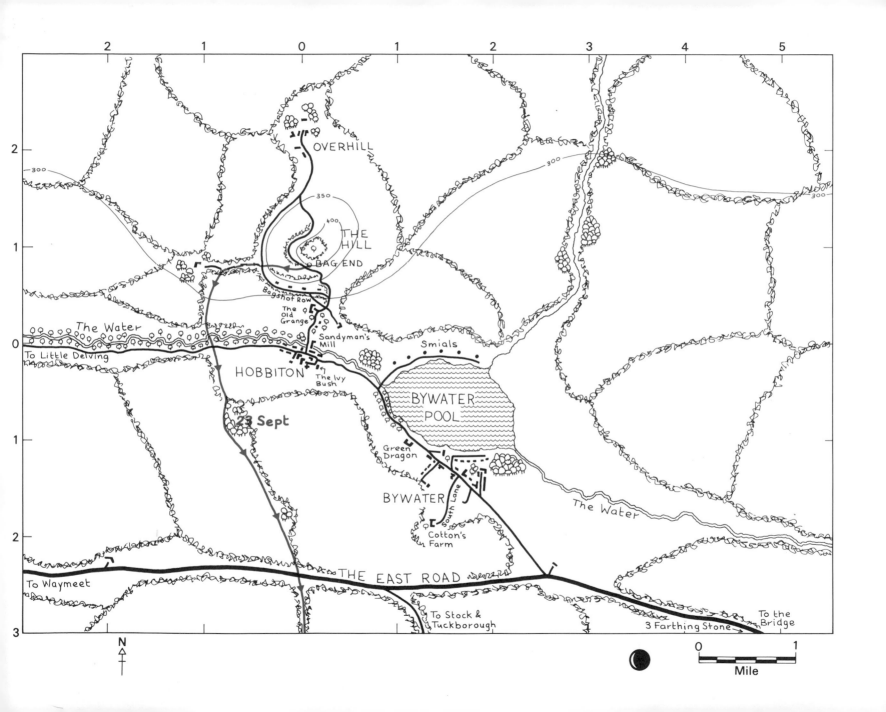

3. Green Hill Country

The travellers had supper under some birches after walking 'for about three hours' (Three is Company; Bk 1); say 8 or 9 miles. This must have been three hours in all, not just since crossing the Water, as they reached their first camping place at 'nearly midnight' and had started out soon after sunset, around 7 p.m. at that time of year. One has reason to suppose that the seasons, and therefore the times of sunrise and sunset, were approximately the same in the Shire as those now applicable in England.

I reckon that they did not travel more than about 14 or 15 miles that first evening.

There was 'a patch of fir-wood' just beyond the top of the hill after they had passed through 'a deeply cloven track between tall trees'. The stream dived under the road at the bottom of the hollow.

They started after ten o'clock next morning and after 'some miles' – perhaps 7 or 8 – they came to a steeper hill with a view ahead, where they lunched. (Three is Company; Bk 1.)

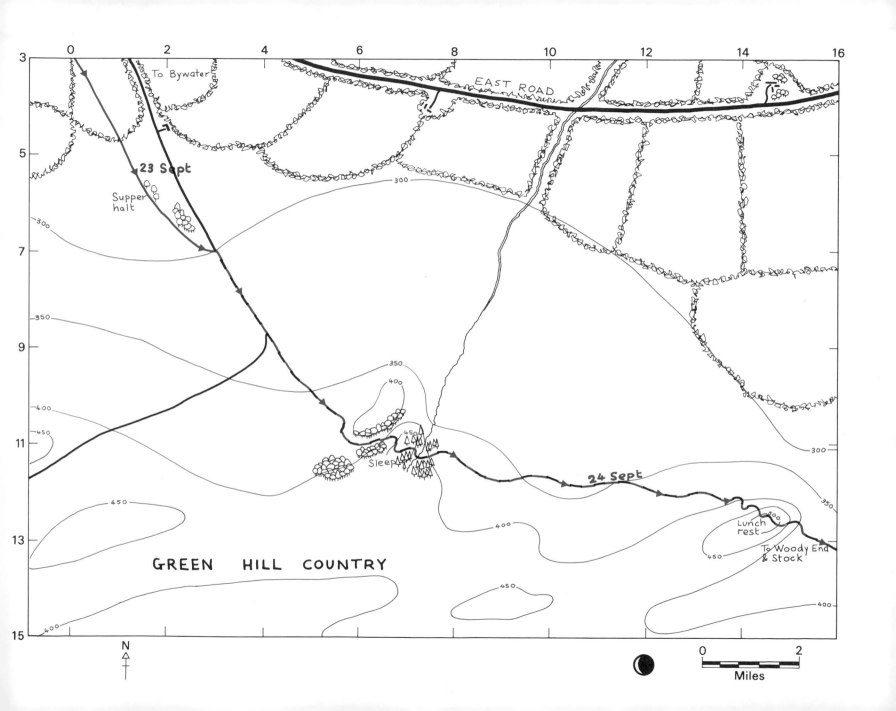

4. Woody End

The travellers started late after lunch and were delayed when they had to hide from the Black Rider on a long straight level stretch of road. It was dusk when they stopped for supper – say 6 miles from the lunch halt – and perhaps another 2 miles before they met the Elves, when they still had, as the Elves told them, 'some miles to go' before they reached the greensward where they spent the night. So it was a much longer and more strenuous day for them, more than 20 miles in all, I reckon, but at least they managed to fit in two suppers – always a welcome treat for Hobbits.

The greensward was on the edge of a steep bluff overlooking the Stockbrook.

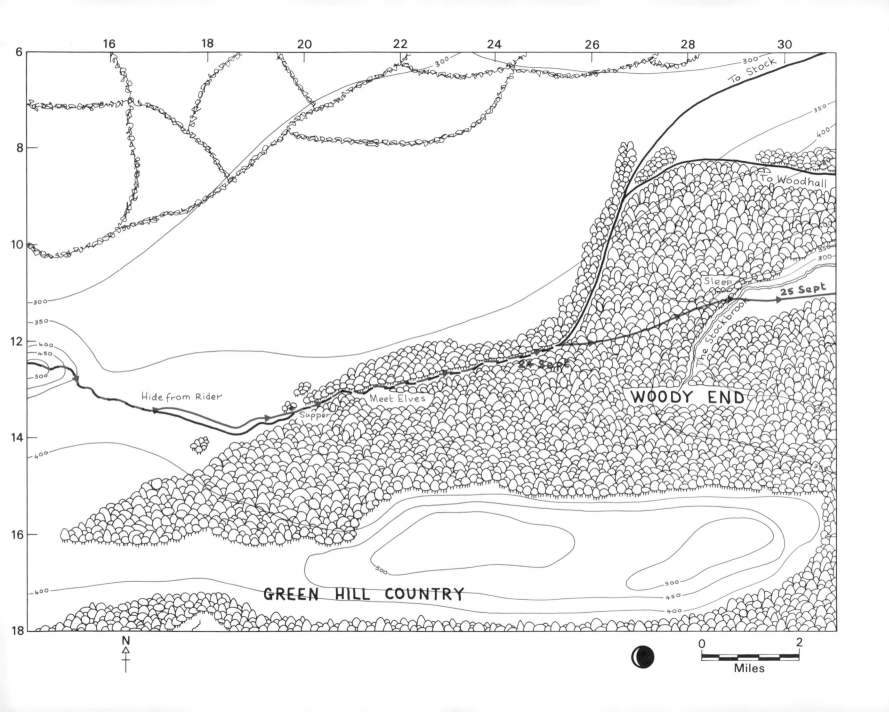

5. Maggot's Farm

Frodo decided to cut across country to the Ferry, which at that point was 18 miles south-east in a straight line through open country after passing through a belt of trees. I make it more nearly east-south-east, in fact, but in any case it must have been south of due east. If they had succeeded in keeping to their line they would certainly have run into difficulties in the marsh, as Pippin warned Frodo.

They lost their way, however, and no doubt started walking in a circle in the woods, as one does when one is lost, so that they came out of the wood much too far south. By now I reckon they had travelled some 8 or 9 miles – 2 of them after the lunch halt. (A Short Cut to Mushrooms; Bk 1.) At this point the Ferry was 'to their left'. Time was getting on and they would have made as straight as possible for the Ferry, bearing somewhat left, until they struck the lane leading to Maggot's farm.

If the Causeway ran due south here, parallel to the river, as it appears to do in the map of the Shire in *The Fellowship of the Ring*, we have a problem. We are told that the lane from Maggot's farm to the road was 'a mile or two' and from the point where it joined the Causeway to the Ferry 'somewhat over 5 miles'. We also know that the lane to the Ferry was only 100 yards long, though the Shire map makes it nearer 2 miles. Consequently, if the Causeway ran due south at this point Maggot's farm would have had to be much too far east to have been anywhere near the Hobbits' route, and I do not think they would have gone far out of their direct way – particularly to the south – and especially as they were nervous of trespassing.

I have therefore assumed that there must have been a considerable westward swing in the Causeway – perhaps to bring it to the 'island' on which I have assumed Rushey to have been built. (A Short Cut to Mushrooms; Bk 1.)

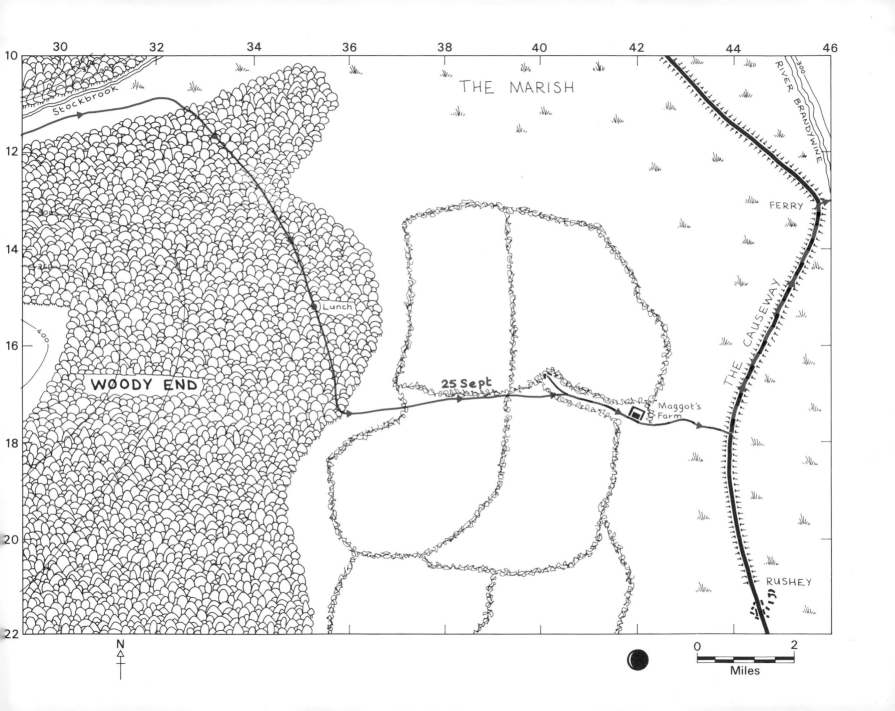

THE MARISH

Stockbrook

RIVER BRANDYWINE

300

300

FERRY

Lunch

THE CAUSEWAY

WOODY END

25 Sept

Maggot's Farm

400

RUSHEY

N

0 2
Miles

6. Brandywine Bridge to Bree

Part of the ground covered is to be found in the map, *A Part of the Shire*, but I depart from this on the course of the Causeway road between Bucklebury Ferry and Rushey. My reasons for the change were given in the Note to Map 5.

There is another point, namely the distance from Brandywine Bridge to the Ferry. When the Black Rider reached the Ferry, Merry says that to get to them he would either have to swim the river or go 20 miles north to the Bridge. (A Conspiracy Unmasked; Bk 1.) I have assumed that he meant 20 miles in all – 10 miles north to the Bridge and 10 miles south on the other side. To assume that the Ferry was 20 miles south of the Bridge won't work, as then the Hedge, which is said to be 'well over 20 miles from end to end', would have had to be more like 40 or 50 miles long if it was to end at the confluence of the river Withywindle, as stated. (A Conspiracy Unmasked; Bk 1.)

I have put Rushey, like Stock, on an 'island' in the Marsh. I have also marked the avenue of trees along the East Road between the Bridge and Bree, and the hedge which misled the travellers when they saw it from the Barrow-downs. (Fog on the Barrow-downs; Bk 1.)

The Greenway bent a little east at the point where it goes off the map, and entered the defile of Andrath, between the Barrow-downs and the South Downs. (The Hunt for the Ring; *Unfinished Tales*.)

Details of the route can be seen in Map 5 and Maps 7 to 9.

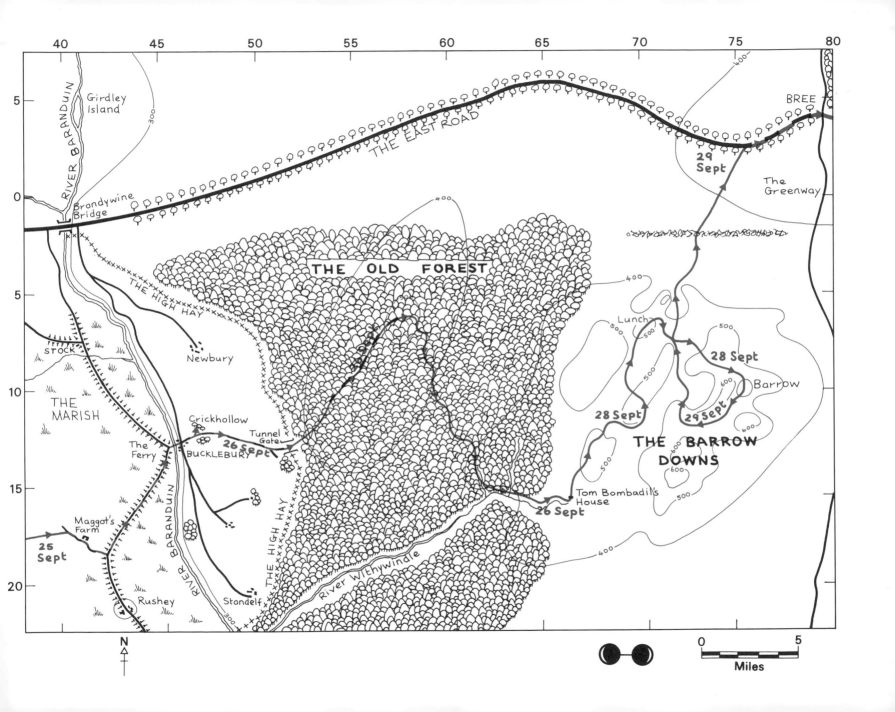

7. Bucklebury and the Hedge

After the Hobbits crossed the Ferry and came up the steep bank on the other side, they passed Buck Hill and Brandy Hall on their left (A Conspiracy Unmasked; Bk 1) before reaching the main road from Brandywine Bridge. They then went north for about half a mile along this road before turning off to Crickhollow which was reached through a narrow gate in a thick hedge.

There were still a lot of Smials in Bucklebury, and I have shown these along the north-west side of the hill.

Incidentally this was another day when the Hobbits had two suppers.

It seems possible that the lane to Crickhollow led on to some farm or homestead near the Hedge, and that it was this path along which they travelled the next morning, after making their way through the spinney behind the house, turning off it to ride left along the Hedge to the Tunnel Gate. They had been riding fairly slowly for about an hour by then, so it must have been about 4 or 5 miles. (The Old Forest; Bk 1.)

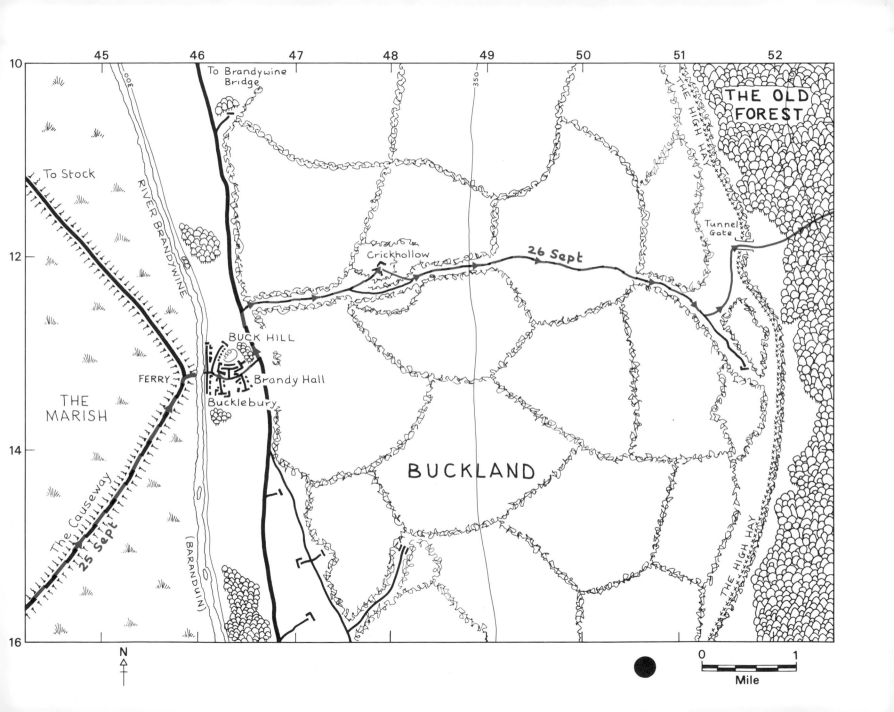

THE OLD
FOREST

To Brandywine
Bridge

THE HIGH HAY

Tunnel
Gate

To Stock

RIVER BRANDYWINE

300

350

Crickhollow

26 Sept

12

BUCK HILL

350

Brandy Hall

FERRY

Bucklebury

THE
MARISH

BUCKLAND

The Causeway
25 Sept

(BARANDUIN)

14

THE HIGH HAY

N

Mile

0   1

8. The Old Forest

There was a cleared space on the other side of the Tunnel, and after entering the trees and climbing for a bit they reached the Bonfire Glade. Beyond this they climbed again to the bald top of the hill, which they reached about 11 a.m. (The Old Forest; Bk 1.)

They were 'not many miles' from the East Road here (some 9, I reckon, see Map 6) but they were misled by the baleful influence of the forest and switched further and further south and east until they scrambled down a gully to the river Withywindle.

Hobbits, we are told (Of Herbs and Stewed Rabbit; Bk 2), cannot manage more than about 24 miles a day on foot, subject, normally, to extended meal breaks. No doubt their metabolism genuinely required the large amounts of food they ate. This, however, was one of the days when they were all riding ponies and they should have been able to cover some 30-35 miles. With all the difficulties they came across, however, I do not think they managed more than about 25 miles.

Tom Bombadil's house was on the west side of a hill (Fog on the Barrow-downs; Bk 1) which was apparently just called 'Hill' (The Old Forest; Bk 1), just as Bag End was on a hill just called 'The Hill'. It was just outside the eaves of the Forest which ran sharply north from there.

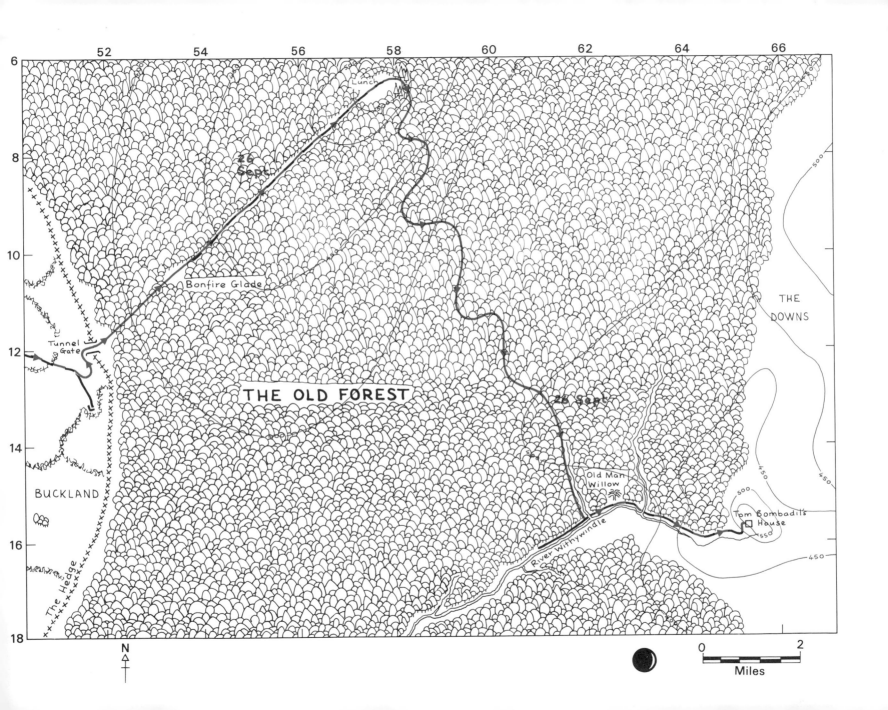

52 54 56 58 60 62 64 66

6

8

10

12

14

16

18

26
Sept.

Bonfire Glade

Tunnel
Gate

Lunch

THE OLD FOREST

BUCKLAND

The Hedge

26 Sept

Old Man
Willow

River Withywindle

Tom Bombadil's
House

THE
DOWNS

500

500

450

450

550

450

N

0   2
Miles

9. The Barrow-downs

I believe the slopes of the Barrow-downs must have started *within* the borders of the Forest and have run up quite steeply on that side, because if there had been a valley or flat space between the trees and the hills there would have been no need for the Hobbits to wander into the downs at all; they could have ridden due north and avoided them.

They started north from Tom Bombadil's house (Fog on the Barrow-downs; Bk 1) and then up and down and round the hills. They made another overlong lunch halt in a spot from which they could see the gate-like opening on the north side of the downs, and also the misleading line of bushes which they thought was the avenue of trees bordering the East Road.

When they got lost in the fog they tried to bear north towards the 'gate' but wandered, in fact, towards the east where the downs were higher, until Frodo found himself facing south on the Barrow-wights hill. Next morning Tom Bombadil led them west and then north to the northern gap and away from the downs, past the dike and bushes and so onto the road. (Fog on the Barrow-downs; Bk 1.)

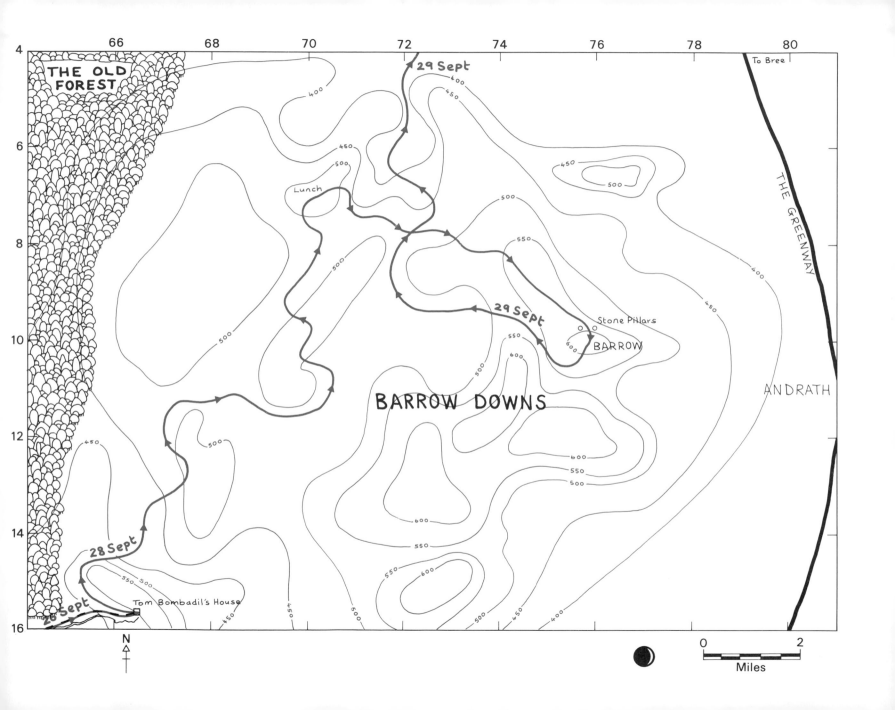

THE OLD FOREST

400

450

500

450

500

Lunch

29 Sept

450

500

550

400

500

29 Sept

550

Stone Pillars

BARROW

600

550

600

BARROW DOWNS

500

ANDRATH

600

550

500

600

550

500

28 Sept

450

500

550

600

28 Sept

Tom Bombadil's House

450

500

550

600

450

500

400

To Bree

THE GREENWAY

N

0   2
Miles

10. Bree

At the point where they reached the East Road and parted from Tom Bombadil, it was running south-west to north-east, and they were about four miles from Bree. (Fog on the Barrow-downs; Bk 1.)

Bree faced west under the steep side of Bree Hill. There was a semi-circular dike and hedge on the west side, with one gate to the west, leading to the cross-roads where the Greenway crossed the East Road, and a second gate to the south. The inn backed onto the hillside and looked west – it must have been just about where the road swung south from the west gate to the south gate. (At the Sign of *The Prancing Pony*; Bk 1.)

It is clear that Chetwood reached far enough south to stretch across the road out of Bree. (A Knife in the Dark; Bk 1.) Staddle was on the other side of the hill from Bree, Combe in a deep valley further east and Archet on the edge of Chetwood. (At the Sign of *The Prancing Pony*; Bk 1.)

There are some who maintain that Archet was on the *northern* edge of Chetwood, but I cannot agree. That would put it some 30 miles away and it is clearly stated that it was hidden in the trees beyond Combe and when the travellers left the road to go north into Chetwood they went first towards Archet but then bore right and passed it on their left. (A Knife in the Dark; Bk 1.) In any case it was close enough for some of the villagers to see the travellers off from Bree, and Breeland must have been a small and close community.

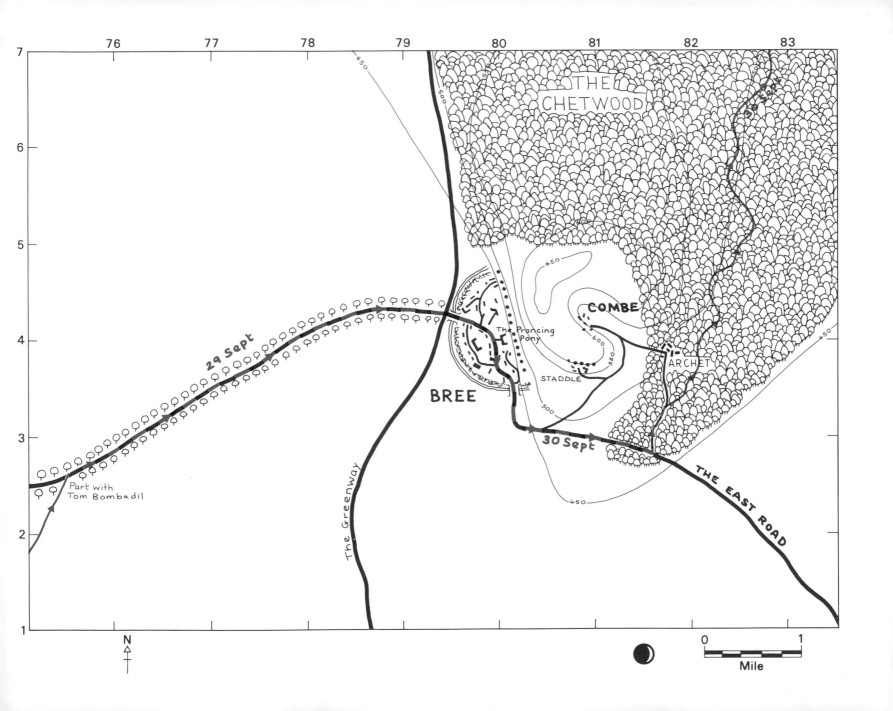

11. Bree to Weathertop

At this point I must note what I believe to be a real discrepancy in the text itself. In Bree (At the Sign of *The Prancing Pony*; Bk 1) Aragorn tells Sam that Weathertop is halfway to *Rivendell*. I am sure that this was a slip of the tongue and that he meant halfway to *The Last Bridge*. Everything falls into place on this assumption, since the travellers took 7 days between Bree and Weathertop (involving a detour to the north) and 7 days from Weathertop to the Bridge (with Frodo in a wounded condition and unable to hurry) while there was a *further* stretch of 7 days from the Bridge to Rivendell. Aragorn was well aware of the distance, as he said later (A Knife in the Dark; Bk 1), when they reached Weathertop, that it would then take them 14 days to the Ford of Bruinen although it normally took him only 12. I have tried to construct a map in which the original statement would work, but it would involve carrying the road from Bree to Weathertop down in so vast a southward loop – over 200 miles – that it would run far south of the South Downs, and as the loop was merely to avoid the marshes (A Knife in the Dark; Bk 1) this is not plausible. I have therefore gone on the assumption that he meant to say 'The Last Bridge'.

Aragorn took his companions a fairly long way north within Chetwood before turning east, and only emerged from the wood on the third day. This was probably not only as a precaution against pursuit but also because he knew that the marsh was impassable further south. The travellers spent two nights in Midgewater and then the land began to rise again. They went straight on and then south along the foot of the hills. (A Knife in the Dark; Bk 1.)

The Forsaken Inn was a day's journey east of Bree along the East Road. (A Knife in the Dark; Bk 1.)

South of Bree the Greenway passed through the defile of Andrath on its way to Tharbad and the south, and was later joined by the road from Sarn Ford. (See Map 49.)

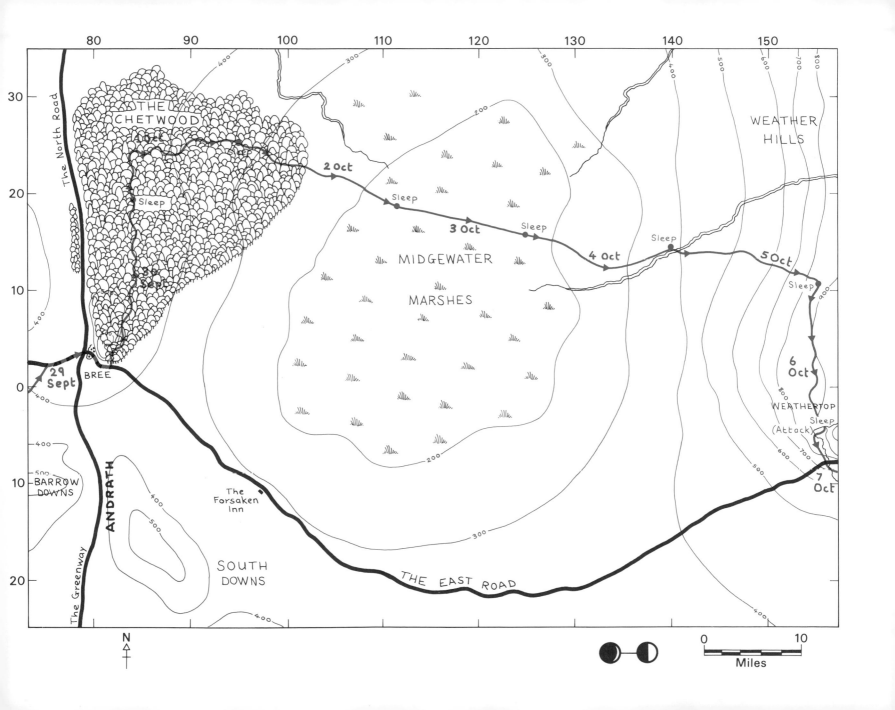

12. Weathertop

The Weather Hills rose up to nearly 1000 feet and ran north to south. Weathertop itself was the highest, and the dell in which they sheltered was on its west flank and only half an hour's climb from the top. (A Knife in the Dark; Bk 1.) The ruins on the top were those of Amon Sûl. (Council of Elrond; Bk 1; and The Northern Kingdom and the Dúnedain; Appendix A, Bk 3.)

There was a small stream in the dell which I have made drain south instead of into the marsh. I have no specific warrant for this but it seemed to me likely that there would be some tributaries flowing into the Hoarwell from the west as well as from the east, and that if so they would rise either on Weathertop or on the South Downs. Since one stream was actually mentioned as rising on Weathertop I have assumed that it was one of these.

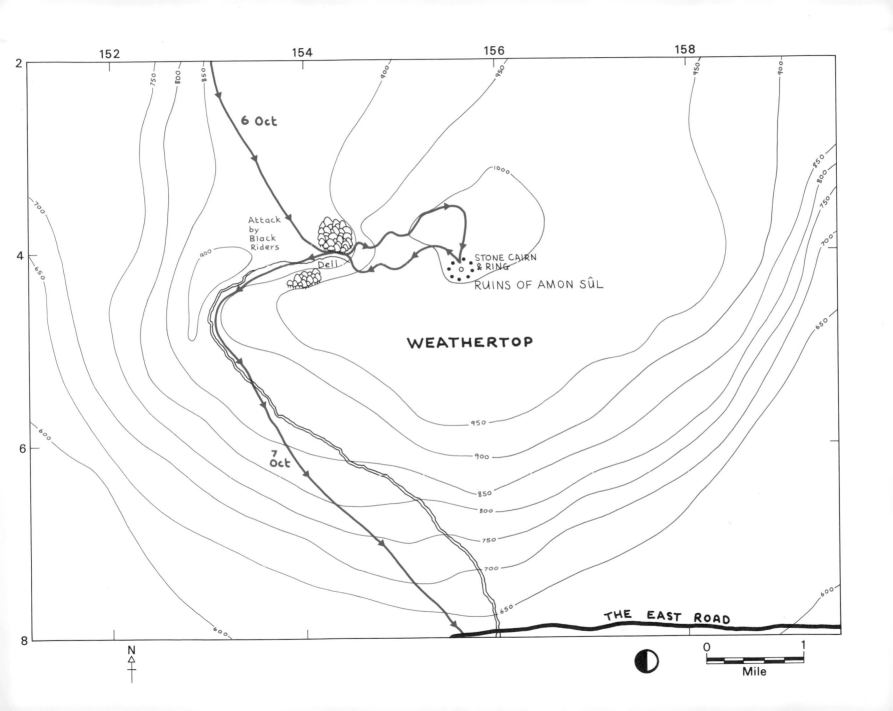

13. Weathertop and the Trollshaws

Between Weathertop and the Hoarwell the travellers were making very slow progress because of Frodo's wound – probably no more than 15–18 miles a day. When they reached the eastern side of the dry valley they were crossing (to avoid the northerly loop of the road here) they climbed a long low slope. (Flight to the Ford; Bk 1.) It must have ended up as a noticeable hill, because from the top they were able to see a long way. In fact they saw not only the Hoarwell but also, in the far distance, a second river, the Loudwater. This must have been much closer than it appears in the maps of Middle-earth which are included in the three books of *The Lord of the Rings*. I believe, in fact, that the Loudwater must have made a sharp westward turn before swinging south again to join the Hoarwell. As shown in the map the two would have been some 100 miles apart and the hill would have had to have been a high mountain for it to have been visible. Furthermore Aragorn says that the road runs *along* the Loudwater for many miles before the Ford. (Flight to the Ford; Bk 1.)

The area must have been wooded, as it is called not only the Ettenmoors but also the Trollshaws. The hills got higher and more difficult as the travellers penetrated them.

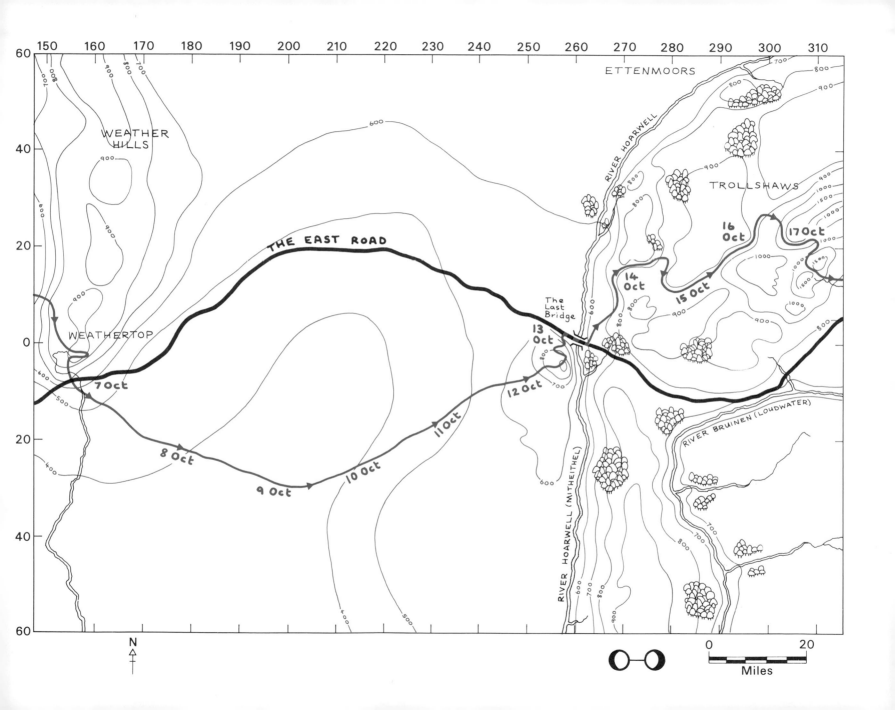

14. The Trollshaws

There must have been even more woods among the Trollshaws than I have drawn, but this one is described in the text. (Flight to the Ford; Bk 1.) The travellers climbed down the southern side of the ridge and soon found a path; they followed this through dark woods until it turned sharply left round the rocky shoulder of the hill and there they found a Troll-hole with a broken door.

The path turned to the right and went on into the woods again, and in a clearing they found the Stone Trolls. After lunch they went on for a few miles until they came out onto the road, and a short while later they were overtaken by Glorfindel.

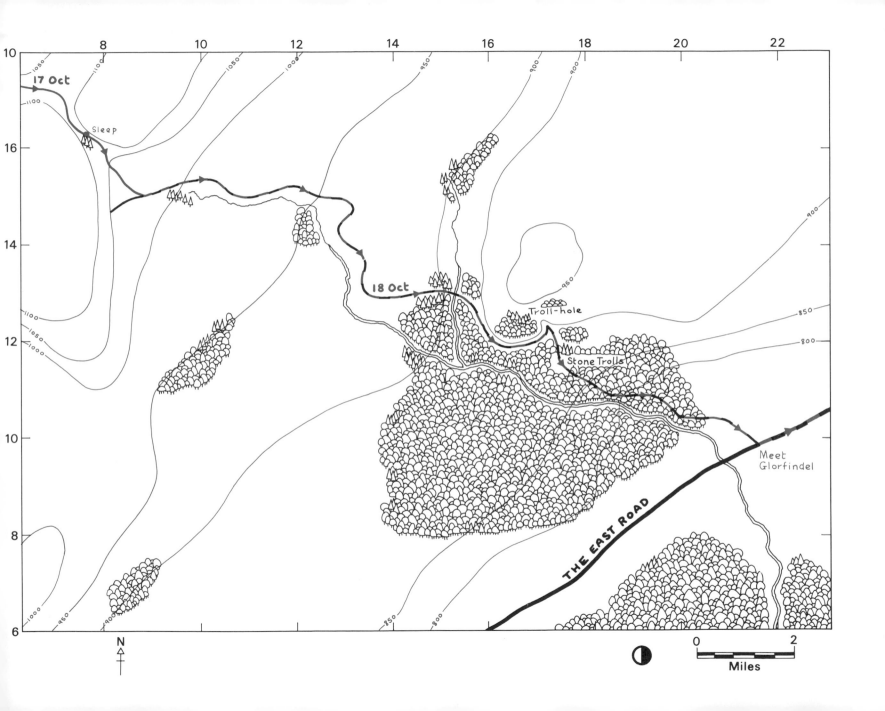

17 Oct

Sleep

18 Oct

Troll-hole

Stone Trolls

Meet
Glorfindel

THE EAST ROAD

N

0   2
Miles

15. To the Ford

The road had taken a northward swerve when the travellers joined it, and was clinging close to the hills. (Flight to the Ford; Bk 1.) I have assumed that this was to avoid a steepish hill and perhaps a thick wood to the south of the road between it and the river.

The stretch between the camp on the high ridge above the Troll-hole and the Ford took three days and was a long and difficult one. On the first day Glorfindel made them push on through the night and by the time they were allowed 5 hours rest they must have covered some 30 miles in all. The next day they covered almost 20 miles and slept at a point where the road turned right and started running down to the river. On the third day they went downhill and passed through a deep cutting with tall pine trees before the road ran out for 'a long flat mile' to the Ford. In all they must have done over 70 miles in the three days. (Flight to the Ford; Bk 1.)

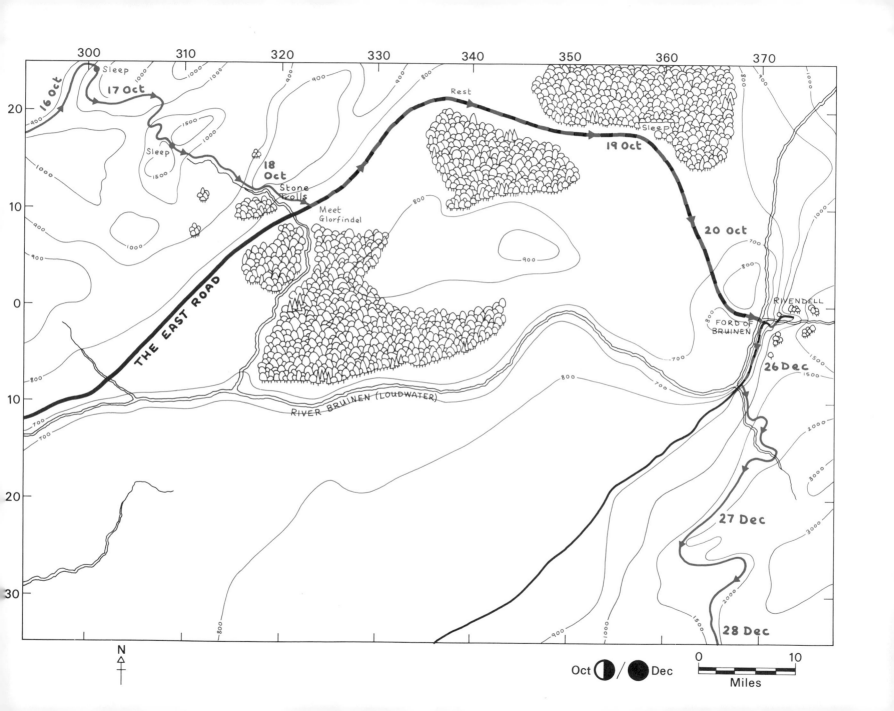

16. Rivendell

The map of Rivendell is based on the three drawings made of it by Tolkien. The road winds up from the Ford and then down again on the south side of the ravine. The cliffs were extremely steep and the gorge narrow to the west of the house but the valley opened out as it went east. The house itself lay on the further side of the stream and was reached by a bridge. There were trees at the top of the cliffs as well as in the valley itself.

The path I have marked running east up the valley from Rivendell is the route taken by Bilbo and the Dwarves on their way to the High Pass.

Frodo and the Companions took the road almost back to the Ford before turning south across rough country. (Flight to the Ford; Bk 1; The Ring Goes South; Bk 1.)

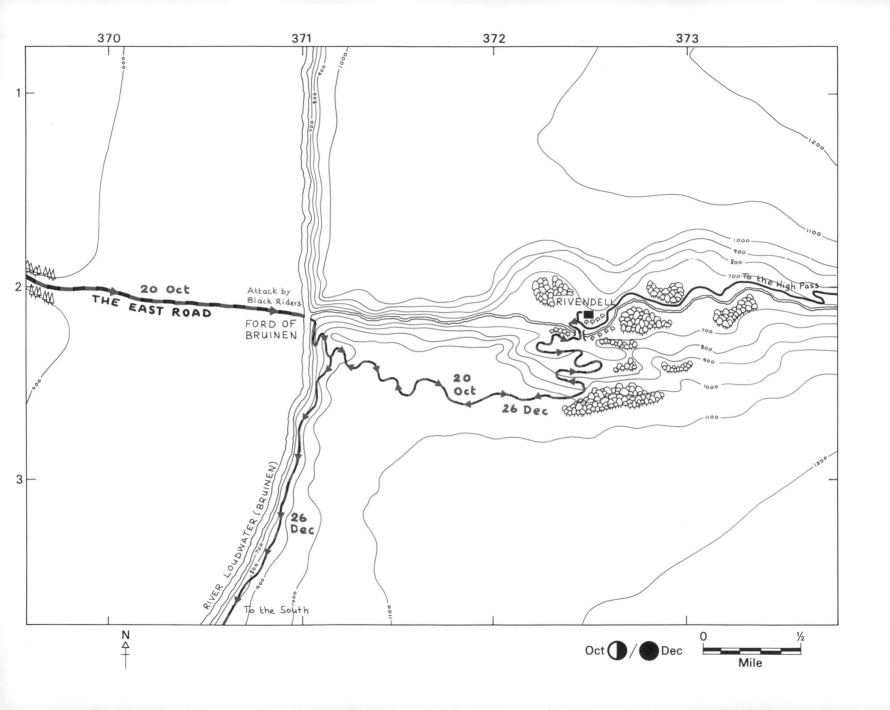

370   371   372   373

1

20 Oct

THE EAST ROAD

Attack by
Black Riders

FORD OF
BRUINEN

RIVENDELL

To the High Pass

2

20
Oct

26 Dec

3

RIVER LOUDWATER (BRUINEN)

26
Dec

To the South

N

Oct ◑ / ● Dec

0   ½

Mile

17. The Misty Mountains

There must once have been some sort of path leading south from Rivendell along the foothills of the Misty Mountains at least as far as Eregion, since Elves dwelt there too. (The Ring Goes South; Bk 1.) Possibly it went on to join the Old North Road between Tharbad and the Gap of Rohan. (See Map 49.) The travellers came up this way on their road home from Minas Tirith when their adventures were over.

On their outward way, however, the Companions avoided this path, so as to keep out of sight. (The Ring Goes South; Bk 1.) It took them a fortnight to travel between Rivendell and Eregion – a distance of 135 miles as the crow flies – giving an average of less than 10 miles progress a day, or rather night, as they walked mainly in the late evenings. They were covering broken country in the dark, and the pony, Bill, might well have slowed them up on the steep bits, although he was useful as a load-carrier.

The mountains bent westwards as they went; more so, in my opinion, than appears in the maps of Middle-earth, especially south of the Redhorn Pass. Frodo said that they then seemed to 'stand across the path' that the Companions were taking. (The Ring Goes South; Bk 1.)

I have assumed the existence of a stream running through Eregion to join the Sirannon before it flowed on down to the Hoarwell. In the old days Eregion was a fruitful land, so I imagine there must have been water there.

The travellers struck the old path running up over Redhorn Pass and down into Dimrill Dale. This path presumably branched off the path going up the Sirannon to Moria Gate.

The three peaks here, Caradhras, Celebdil and Fanuidhol (which is just off this map to the south-west, but is shown on Map 49), were the highest in the range and there were no other passes south of this until the Gap of Rohan. (The Ring Goes South; Bk 1.)

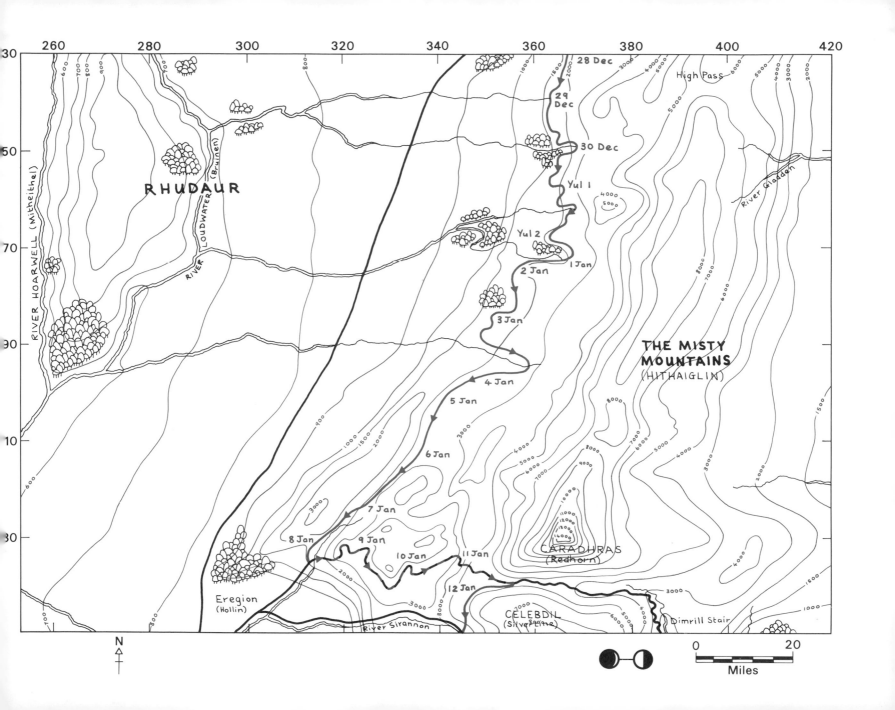

18. Redhorn Gate Pass and Moria

The Redhorn Gate Pass was to the south of Caradhras and the cliff wall beneath which they passed was to their left, with a deep ravine on their right. (The Ring Goes South; Bk 1.) When they turned back, Gandalf led them south, not along the path by which they had come. (A Journey in the Dark; Bk 1.)

When they camped for the night (and were attacked by wolves) he told the Companions that the Moria Gate was 15 miles south-west of Caradhras as the crow flies. The next morning they set off to find the old Dwarf path and finally came upon the dried-up course of the Sirannon. They went on up a deep trough in a narrow valley closed at the end by a towering cliff face that was part of the peak Celebdil. (A Journey in the Dark; Bk 1.) It is shown in the drawing of Moria Gate by Tolkien. The bed of the river was not above the tree line as there were holly trees on the shore of the lake, but it must have been higher than the Great Gates on the other side of the caves, in Dimrill Dale, because of the many flights of stairs within the mountain.

This day was a very long one. Gandalf told them that the whole distance beneath the mountain was 40 miles. On their second day in the passages they covered 15 miles direct, or 20 as the road wound, which brought them nearly to the other side. On the first day (or rather night), therefore, they must have covered nearly 20 miles after passing Durin's Door and this after a good 9 or 10 miles from their overnight camp. Clearly under pressure of extreme danger the Hobbits could manage more than their normal maximum of 24 miles.

It is difficult not to be confusing when one is plotting both caves and the mountains under which they lie. The contour lines here represent the outer surface.

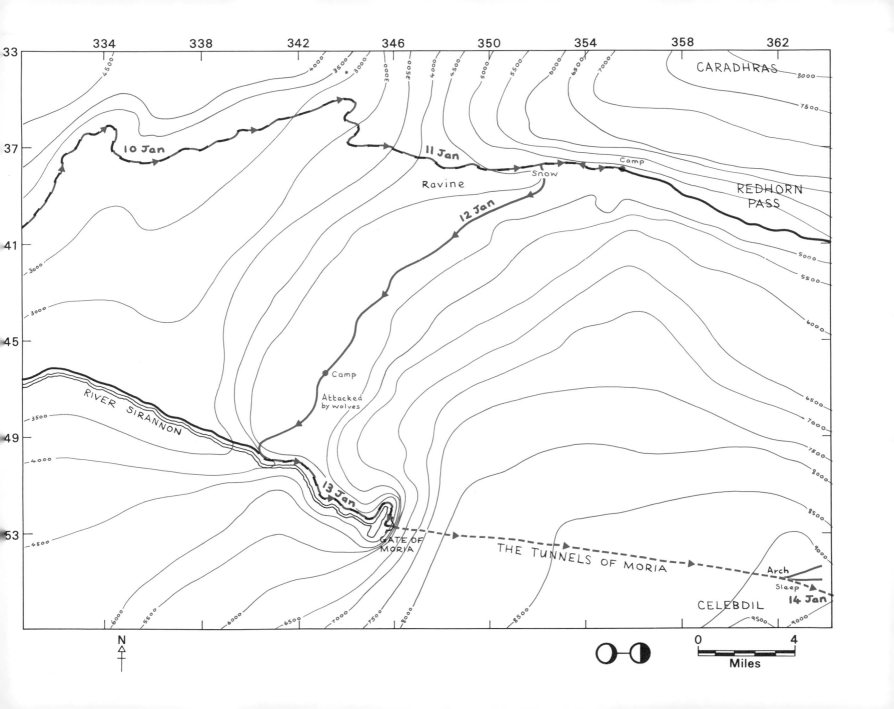

334 338 342 346 350 354 358 362

33

CARADHRAS

8000

7500

10 Jan

11 Jan

37

Ravine

Snow

Camp

REDHORN
PASS

12 Jan

41

5000

5500

6000

45

6500

7000

Camp

7500

Attacked
by wolves

RIVER SIRANNON

8000

49

3500

4000

8500

13 Jan

53

9000

GATE OF
MORIA

THE TUNNELS OF MORIA

Arch

Sleep

14 Jan

CELEBDIL

6000 5500 6000 6500 7500 8000 8500 9500 9000

N

0   4
Miles

19. Moria East Gate and Mirrormere

They slept in the Twenty-first Hall, which must have been high enough up to be very near the surface, as they could see daylight through a shaft. They were above and to the north of the Great Gates. (A Journey in the Dark; Bk 1.) They went north from here and found the Chamber of Mazarbûl – Balin's Tomb – on their right. After their battle with the Orcs here they escaped through the other door and down many flights of stairs covering about a mile in horizontal distance. (The Bridge of Khazad-dûm; Bk 1.)

This led them to the Second Hall, which they entered east of the fiery chasm which had split the floor of the hall. The narrow bridge from which Gandalf fell led from this Hall to a broad stair, along a wide road, through the First Hall to the Great Gates – about a quarter of a mile in all. (The Bridge of Khazad-dûm; Bk 1.) Again there are difficulties when one is plotting both caves and the mountains under which they lie.

After Gandalf fell the others fled this way and finally came through the broken doors and the Great Gates to the open air. There is a picture of the path below the Gates. At some stage down the mountain side the path from the Gates must have joined Dimrill Stair winding down from the Redhorn Pass. The picture shows the path as it crosses the river Dimrill towards the east, and it must, therefore, presumably have run past Durin's Stone down the east side of Mirrormere. (Lothlórien; Bk 1.)

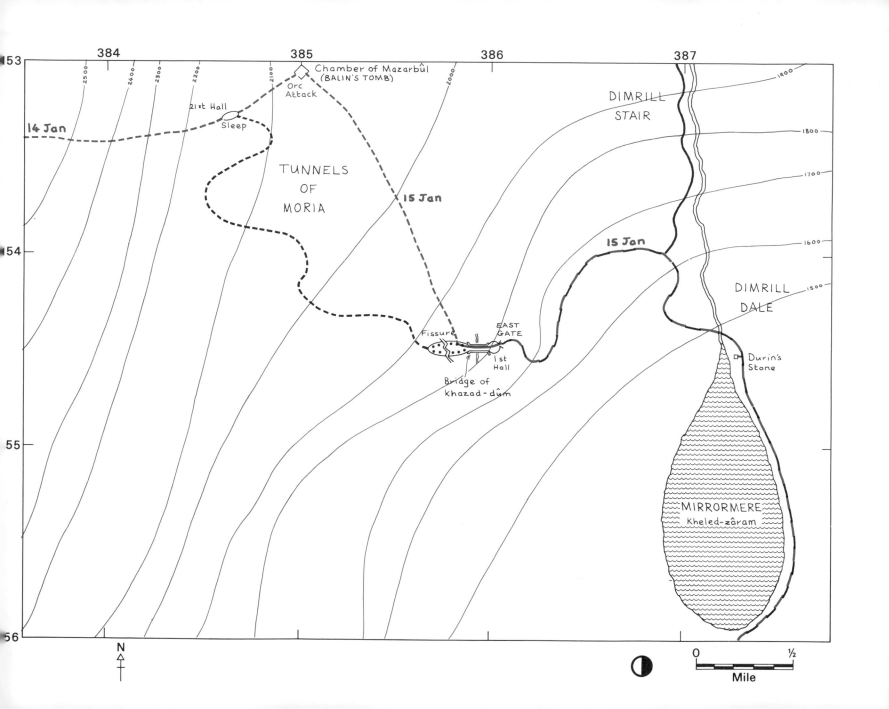

20. East Gate, Dimrill Dale and Nimrodel

After passing the end of the lake they came to the deep well which was the source of the Silverlode, and the path now ran down the right bank of the river. They rested where another stream joined the young river in a dell of fir trees still 'only a few miles' from the Gates, and went on for another three hours – say a further 10 miles – till they came to the Golden Wood. They were now 15 miles from the Gates. After another mile they came to the junction of the Nimrodel, waded across it and went up it, past the falls, till they found some trees where they proposed to sleep and were surprised by the elves.

Incidentally this was another day when the Hobbits managed to get two suppers. (Lothlórien; Bk 1.)

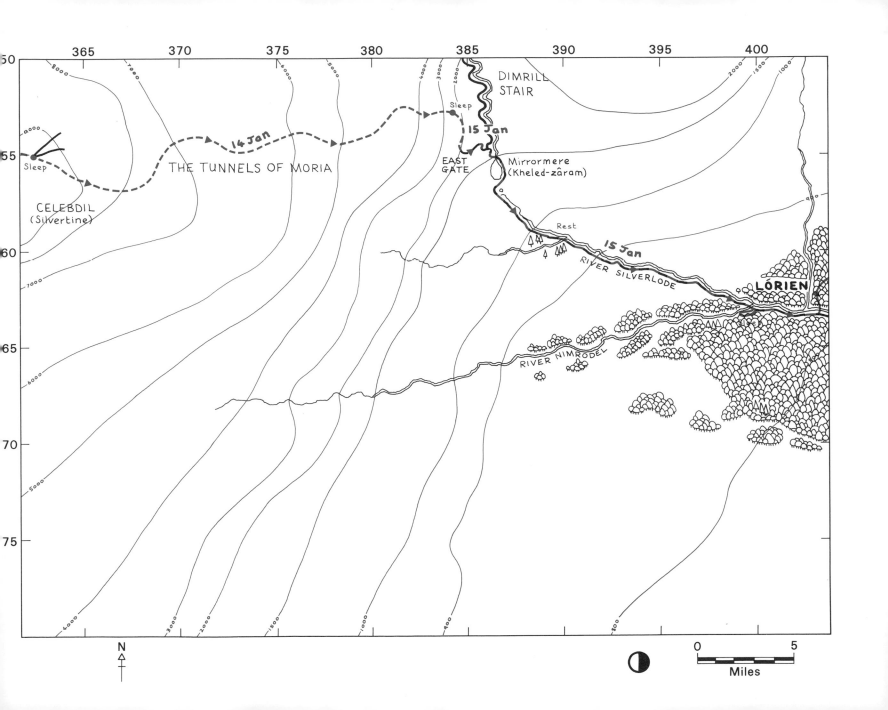

21. Lórien

Trees bordered the Anduin on both sides of the point where the Silverlode (also known as the Celebrant, literally silver-course) flowed into it. Mallorn trees grew on both sides of the Silverlode but there were none on the east side of the Anduin. (Farewell to Lórien; Bk 1.)

The old road from Moria ran along the right bank of the Silverlode. Dol Guldur, Sauron's fortress before he moved to Barad-dûr, was just across the Anduin and the old road must have led there. Dol Guldur was visible – or nearly so – from Cerin Amroth, which was on a hill. (Lothlórien; Bk 1.)

Right at the tip of the Naith, where the two rivers joined, was the green lawn of the Tongue, and a little distance up the Silverlode from there was the hythe where the boats were moored. (Farewell to Lórien; Bk 1.)

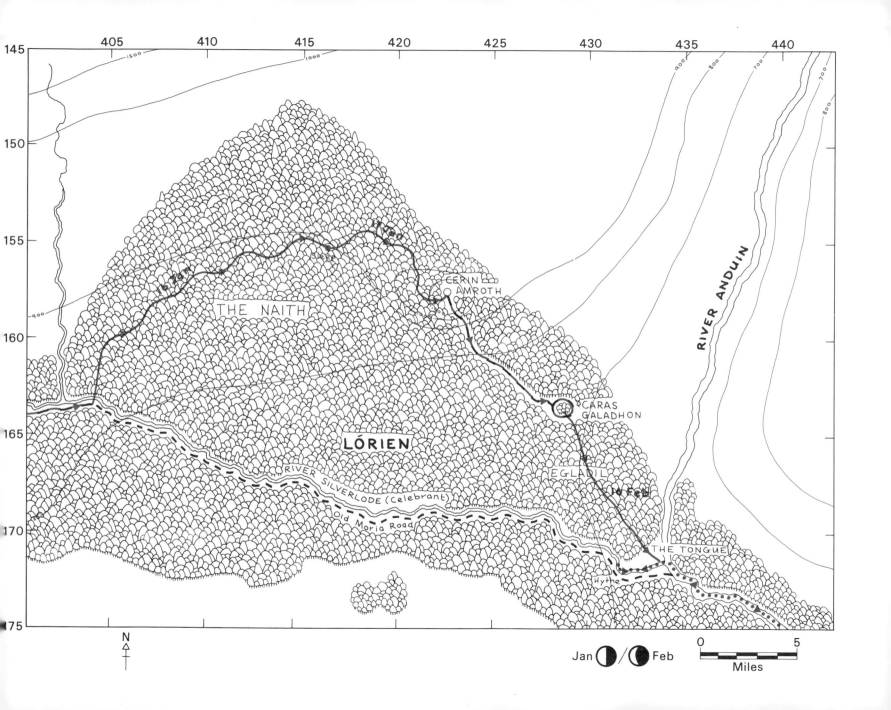

THE NAITH

CERIN
AMROTH

CARAS
GALADHON

LÓRIEN

EGLADIL

RIVER SILVERLODE (Celebrant)

Old Moria Road

THE TONGUE

Hythe

RIVER ANDUIN

N

Jan / Feb

0   5
Miles

22. Anduin and Limlight

The Anduin ran through a steep valley above Lothlórien, which widened out further north where the River Gladden ran into it through great marshes. Here Isildur fell and lost the Ring. (The Shadow of the Past; Bk 1; The Disaster of the Gladden Fields; *Unfinished Tales*.)

Dol Guldur was set on Amon Lanc (Naked Hill), so called because there were no trees on the summit. It was the highest point of this part of Mirkwood. (The Disaster of the Gladden Fields; *Unfinished Tales*.)

Bare trees lined both banks of the Great River downstream of the Silverlode. (It was February.) The travellers slept among the trees for the first two nights. On the third day the trees thinned out and vanished and they were able to see that on the left bank were the wastes of the Brown Lands and on the right wide plains of grass and forests of reeds.

Just before the point where the river Limlight joined the Anduin, Aragorn told them that they were then about 180 miles south of the Southfarthing – say some 240 miles south of Hobbiton. The Limlight rose in Fangorn and was the northern frontier of Rohan.

On the fourth night they camped on an eyot near to the west bank, and Gollum was seen. (The Great River; Bk 1.)

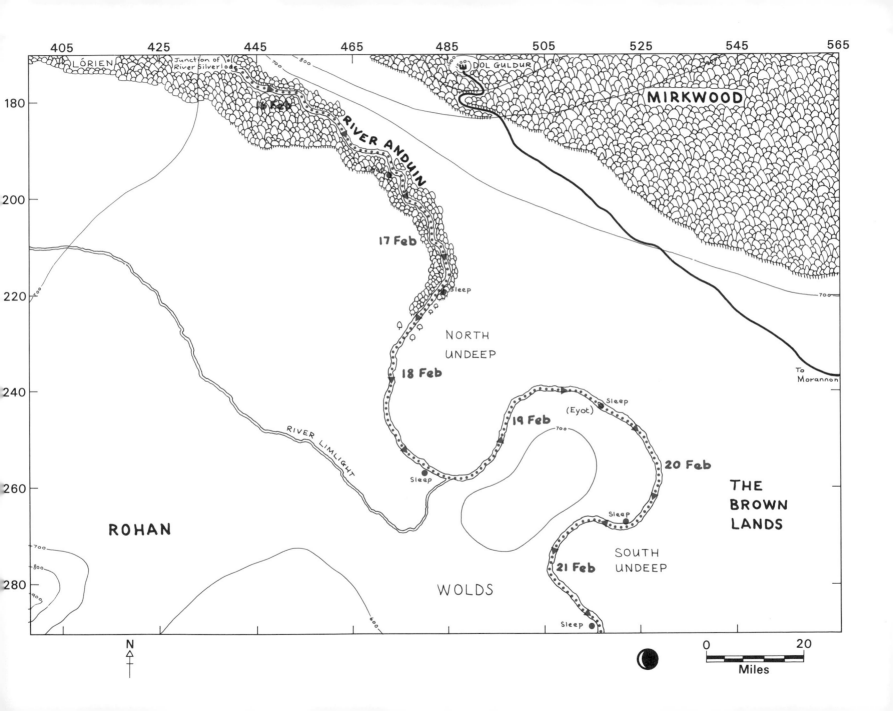

LÓRIEN

Junction of River Silverlode

DOL GULDUR

MIRKWOOD

180

16 Feb

RIVER ANDUIN

200

17 Feb

220

Sleep

NORTH
UNDEEP

700

To Morannon

18 Feb

240

RIVER LIMLIGHT

Sleep

(Eyot)

Sleep

19 Feb

700

20 Feb

260

Sleep

**THE
BROWN
LANDS**

ROHAN

700

800

900

SOUTH
UNDEEP

21 Feb

280

WOLDS

600

Sleep

N

0   20

Miles

23. Anduin and Rohan

After Gollum appeared Aragorn decided that they would have to go faster and they paddled instead of floating with the current. Also they took to travelling by night.

By the eighth night the banks were getting higher and rockier, but Aragorn miscalculated and thought they still had many miles to go before they reached the Rapids of Sarn Gebir. Around midnight, however, they realised that they were entering them. (The Great River; Bk I.)

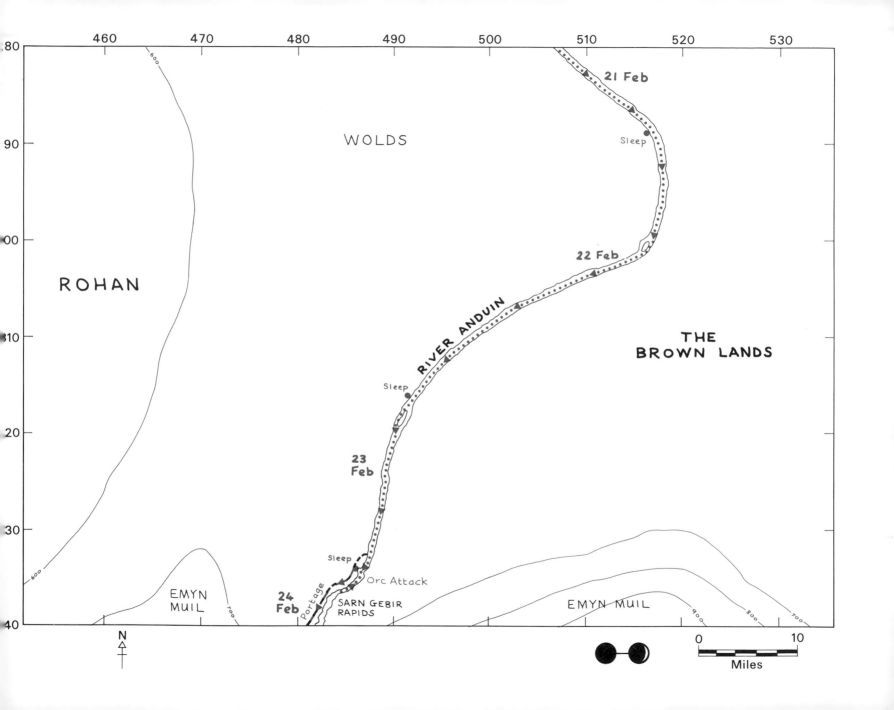

24. Sarn Gebir and Argonath

When the travellers realised that they were in the Rapids, they turned the boats and began to fight their way upstream. The river carried them nearer and nearer to the east bank where they were attacked by Orcs. Finally they managed to get over to the west bank and then upstream a short way until they found a shallow bay where they moored for the rest of the night. (The Great River; Bk 1.)

Next morning they found the Portage Way and carried the boats down it. The Rapids were not much more than a mile long, but they had to make two trips and the task was exhausting and they got no further than the foot of the Rapids that day.

That night they moored in a pool and next day sped along the narrow ravine through the hills of Emyn Muil, finally bending west before they passed through the Gates of Argonath between the Pillars of the Kings and so out into the open lake. There were trees above the steep grey slopes of the hills. (The Great River; Bk 1.)

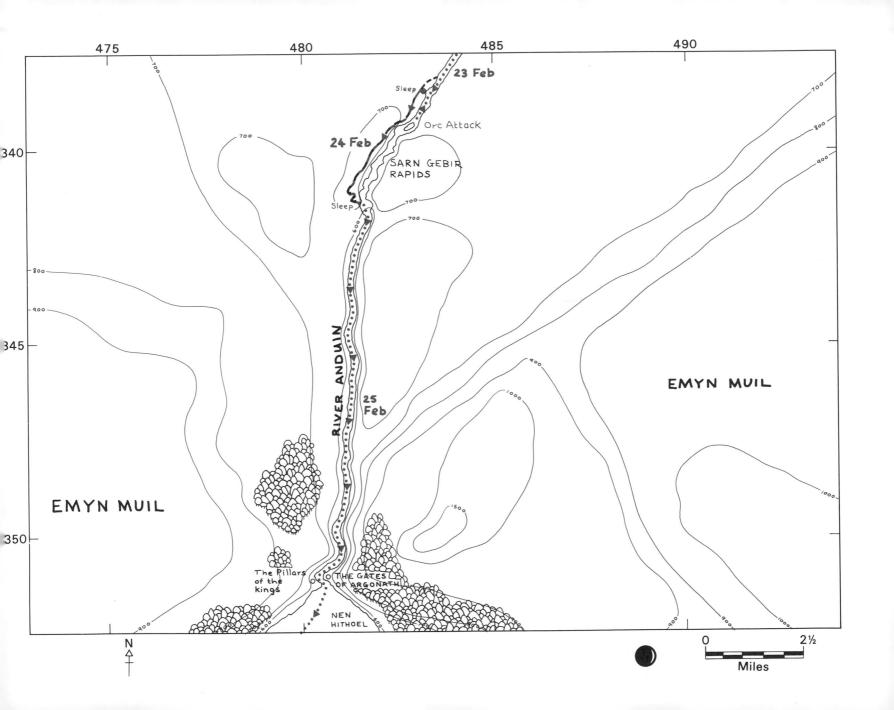

25. Parth Galen

There were three peaks at the south end of the lake, Nen Hithoel, of which Amon Hen was the westernmost, Amon Lhaw the easternmost and the island of Tol Brandir the central one.

Tol Brandir rose steeply to a shelf crowned with trees before rising again to a central peak. The travellers passed to the west of it and landed by a little stream in the lawn of Parth Galen. (The Breaking of the Fellowship; Bk 1.)

The path called the North Stair led down from the lake to the foot of the Falls of Rauros, and had been used for portage in the old days. (The Great River; Bk 1.)

When Frodo sat on the top of Amon Hen (The Mount of Seeing) and put on the Ring, he could see a vast circle reaching from Isengard to Barad-dûr and from the Misty Mountains down to the delta of the Anduin – a radius of a good 300 miles.

As there was so much separate activity over the same ground in this area I have tried to label each track with the name of its maker. The map shows the route by which Frodo and Sam left the others, the course of Boromir's funeral boat, and the various ways taken by the companions when the Orcs seized Merry and Pippin. (The Breaking of the Fellowship; Bk 1.)

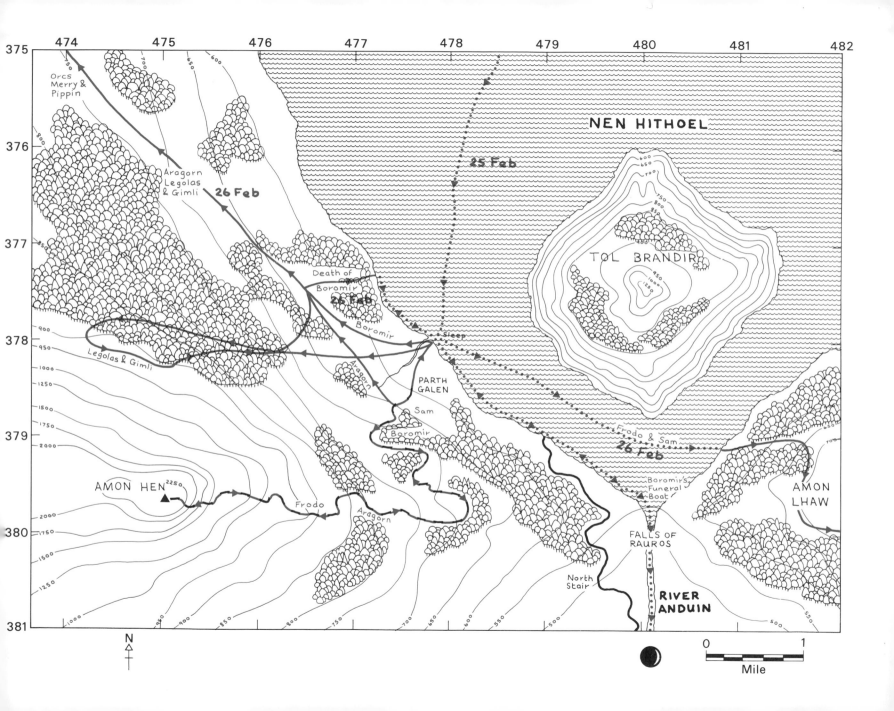

Orcs
Merry &
Pippin

Aragorn
Legolas
& Gimli

26 Feb

NEN HITHOEL

25 Feb

Death of
Boromir

26 Feb

Boromir

Sleep

Legolas & Gimli

Aragorn

PARTH
GALEN

Sam

Boromir

Frodo & Sam

26 Feb

TOL BRANDIR

AMON
LHAW

AMON HEN

Frodo

Aragorn

Boromir's
Funeral
Boat

North
Stair

FALLS OF
RAUROS

**RIVER
ANDUIN**

N

0   1
Mile

26. Eastemnet and Nen Hithoel

The two ridges on the western side of Emyn Muil ran roughly north-south and were steeper on their western sides. (The Riders of Rohan; Bk 2.) Owing to the lie of these ridges I assume that the stream Aragorn came upon after finding the bodies of the Orcs in the hills would have drained into the other stream they passed, which ran down the ravine of the East Wall of Rohan, and we are told that that ran into the Entwash.

The East Wall was a steep ridge on the west side of the Emyn Muil. It rose some 120 feet from a wide and rugged shelf above the plains of the Rohirrim. From the top Legolas saw a great company on foot – clearly the Orcs who had captured Merry and Pippin – some 36 miles ahead.

They scrambled down a deep cleft with a stream in it and ran on across the plain for 36 miles before resting. (The Riders of Rohan; Bk 2.)

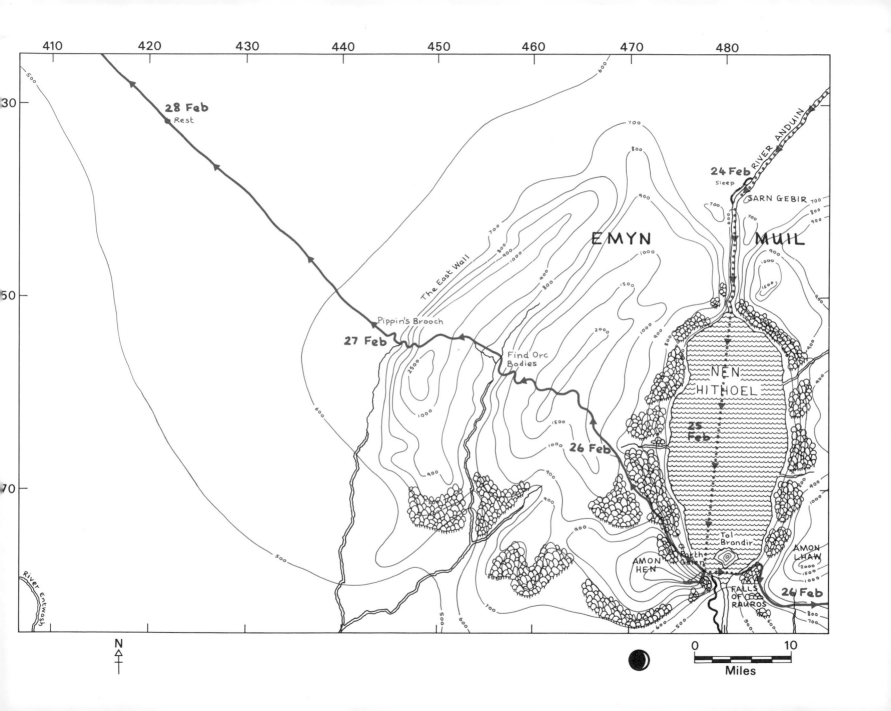

27. The Vale of Entwash

Aragorn, Legolas and Gimli covered 45 leagues in all (135 miles) in their great four-day run, travelling north-west. The last part of this, the downs, stretched for 24 miles Aragorn said, and from the northernmost hill it was 45 miles north-west to the point where the Entwash emerged from the forest of Fangorn. (The Riders of Rohan; Bk 2.) A few pages later in *The Two Towers*, however, it says that from the hill they could see the forest only 30 miles away. There was probably a spur of woods sticking out a little east and south of the river which was nearer than the point where the river emerged.

The marshy land between the downs and the Entwash was about 10 miles wide. The path taken by the Rohirrim led up this east bank of the river after crossing it lower down at the Entwade, because the land to the west of the river was even more marshy. (The Riders of Rohan; Bk 2; The White Rider; Bk 2.)

Deeping Stream must eventually have run into the Entwash.

At the point where the Entwash emerged from Fangorn, Legolas noted that they were almost due west of the point they had reached on the second or third day on the Great River when Aragorn had told them that they were some 180 miles south of the Southfarthing. (The White Rider; Bk 2.)

The stone stair Merry and Pippin climbed (and later also the others) was only 3 or 4 miles from the edge of the forest. (Treebeard; Bk 2.)

The route taken by Merry, Pippin and Treebeard is shown on Map 28, that by Gandalf and his companions on Map 29.

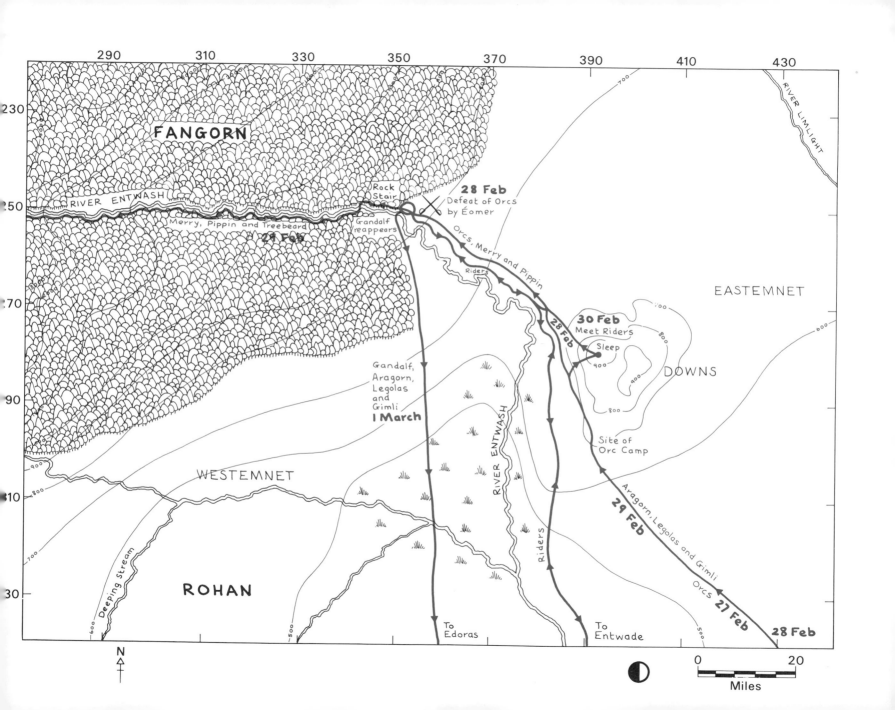

FANGORN

RIVER ENTWASH

Rock Stair

Merry, Pippin and Treebeard
28 Feb

Gandalf reappears

28 Feb
Defeat of Orcs
by Éomer

Orcs, Merry and Pippin

Riders

EASTEMNET

30 Feb
Meet Riders

Sleep

700

800

900

800

800

600

DOWNS

Gandalf,
Aragorn,
Legolas
and
Gimli
1 March

Site of
Orc Camp

WESTEMNET

RIVER ENTWASH

Riders

Aragorn, Legolas and Gimli
29 Feb

Orcs **27 Feb**

28 Feb

900

800

700

Deeping Stream

ROHAN

To Edoras

To Entwade

500

500

N

0   20
Miles

Wellinghall was a long way up the river, nearly at its source. (Treebeard; Bk 2.) Treebeard said he had brought the Hobbits 70,000 Entstrides, but the length of an Entstride is not given. Sam's cousin Hal reported that he had seen an Ent in the Shire, and claimed that his stride was 21 feet long. (A Shadow of the Past; Bk 1.) This would make the distance from the rock stair to Wellinghall nearly 270 miles, so I expect Hal was exaggerating. If Treebeard was 14 ft tall his stride (by comparison with a 3 ft stride for a 6 ft man) was probably something of the order of 6–7 ft. At this rate the distance would be about 80 miles. They probably started from the stair about 10 a.m. and reached Wellinghall at dusk, say 8 hours at 10 miles an hour.

The forest of Fangorn skirted the slopes of Methedras, which was the last peak of the Misty Mountains. (Treebeard; Bk 2.) According to the Book map it was due north of Nan Curunír, the Wizard's Vale.

Leaving Wellinghall the next morning, Treebeard went south and then east into the forest to Derndingle. The Ents left Derndingle in the afternoon going southward down a long fold of the foothills and up onto the high western ridge – high enough to be just above the treeline. They reached the crest after dark and went on down a long ravine into the upper part of the valley. (Treebeard; Flotsam and Jetsam; Bk 2.)

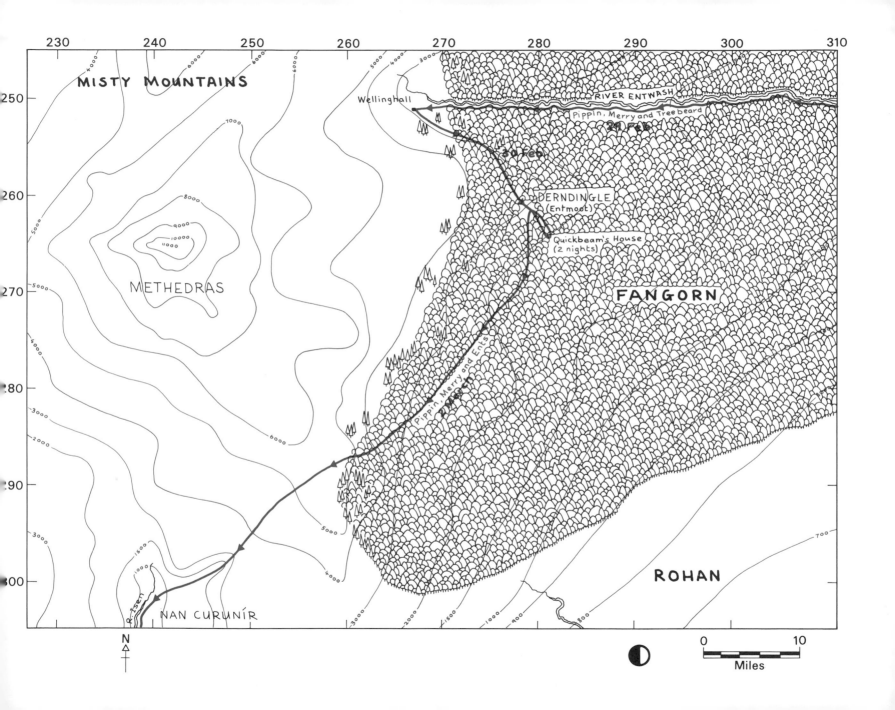

MISTY MOUNTAINS

230 240 250 260 270 280 290 300 310

250

Wellinghall

RIVER ENTWASH

Pippin, Merry and Treebeard

29 Feb

30 Feb

260

DERNDINGLE
(Entmoot)

Quickbeam's House
(2 nights)

270

METHEDRAS

FANGORN

280

Pippin, Merry and Ents

290

300

5000

ROHAN

NAN CURUNÍR

N

0   10
Miles

29. Edoras

The first part of the ride of Gandalf and his companions to Edoras can be seen on Map 27. Shadowfax waded the river and took them due south, through fen and hollow, by a route known only to himself. (The White Rider; Bk 2.)

I make the distance to Edoras nearly 130 miles, which they covered in less than 24 hours. Even allowing for rests, this was a remarkable equine feat and the other horses must have been inspired by Shadowfax.

Edoras was at the point where the Snowbourn emerged from the mountains and turned east to join the Entwash. Four roads met there: the Great West Road to Minas Tirith, the path Éomer and his Riders had taken to the Entwade, the road to the Fords of Isen, and the road south up the valley to Dunharrow. (The King of the Golden Hall; Bk 2.)

When Gandalf and the others set off again with Théoden and his men, they took the road leading north-west along the foothills of the White Mountains. It was more than 40 leagues (120 miles) direct, or say 135 miles by the road. It crossed many swift streams, of which I have plotted two, which, together with Deeping Stream, must have run into the Entwash and helped to fill the marshes along its banks. (Helm's Deep; Bk 2.)

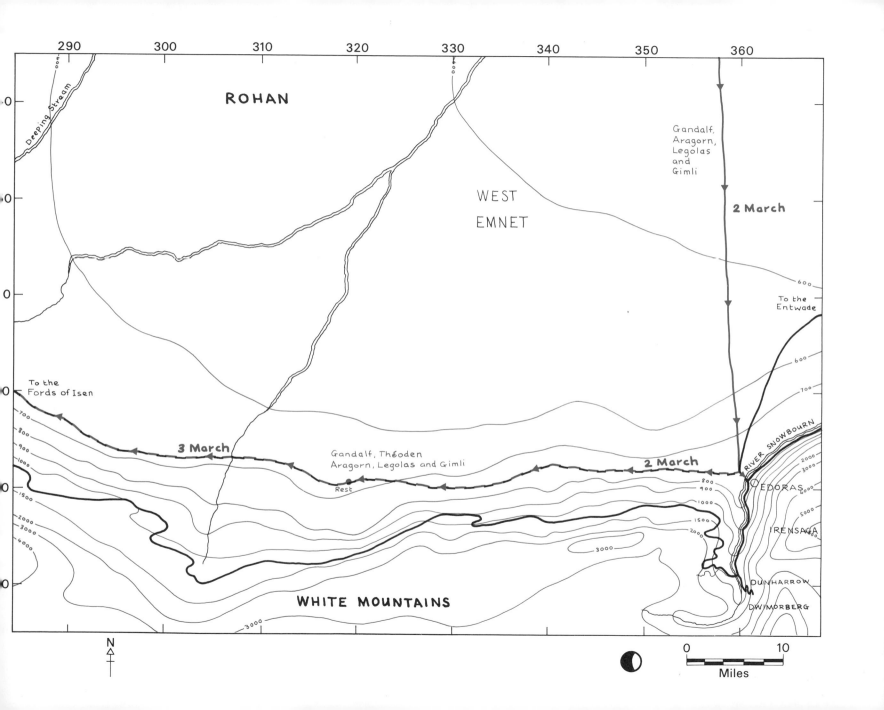

290   300   310   320   330   340   350   360

ROHAN

Deeping Stream

WEST
EMNET

Gandalf,
Aragorn,
Legolas
and
Gimli

2 March

600

To the
Entwade

To the
Fords of Isen

700
800
900
1000

3 March

Gandalf, Théoden
Aragorn, Legolas and Gimli

Rest

2 March

600

700

RIVER SNOWBOURN

800
900
1000
1500
2000

2000
3000
4000
5000
6000

EDORAS

IRENSAGA

1500
2000
3000
4000

3000

1500

2000

3000

DUNHARROW

DWIMORBERG

WHITE MOUNTAINS

3000

N

0   10

Miles

30. Nan Curunír and Deeping-coomb

Nan Curunír, the valley where Isengard was built, is spelt with a G in the Book map, but I have followed the text and spelt it with a C. (Treebeard; The Road to Isengard; Bk 2.)

It was 15 miles from the mouth of Deeping-coomb to the Fords. The road from Edoras approached from the south-east, turning straight west for the last 2 miles before running down a long sloping bank to the river. (The Battles of the Fords of Isen; *Unfinished Tales*.) After crossing the Fords they went east and north to the mouth of the Vale for about 14 miles and camped by the river. They were then some 16 miles from Isengard. (The Road to Isengard; Bk 2.) In the Battles of the Fords of Isen (*Unfinished Tales*) it is said that from the point where the road to Hornburg branched off, it was 90 miles in a straight line to Isengard, but I find that impossible to reconcile with the clear directions given in *The Lord of the Rings*, and noted above. They reached Isengard on 5th March.

The ruined road which I have drawn running west from the Fords led northwards to Tharbad, and in the old days it was the main north–south road. There must also have been some sort of a path, probably on the east side of the Isen, leading to the stronghold on the Adorn, which had been built in the old days by Helm Hammerhand. (The House of Eorl; Appendix A, Bk 3; see also Map 49.)

There was probably no real road leading south on the west side of the Isen, but it was possible to reach Gondor by going down to the sea and turning east. When they failed to cross Redhorn Pass the Companions considered and rejected the idea of travelling this way. (A Journey in the Dark; Bk 1.)

This map also shows the beginning of Gandalf and Pippin's ride to Minas Tirith. They left Isengard on 5th March. The whole course of the ride is shown on Map 33. The route of the ride to Helm's Deep, which preceded the Battle (Map 31), is also given.

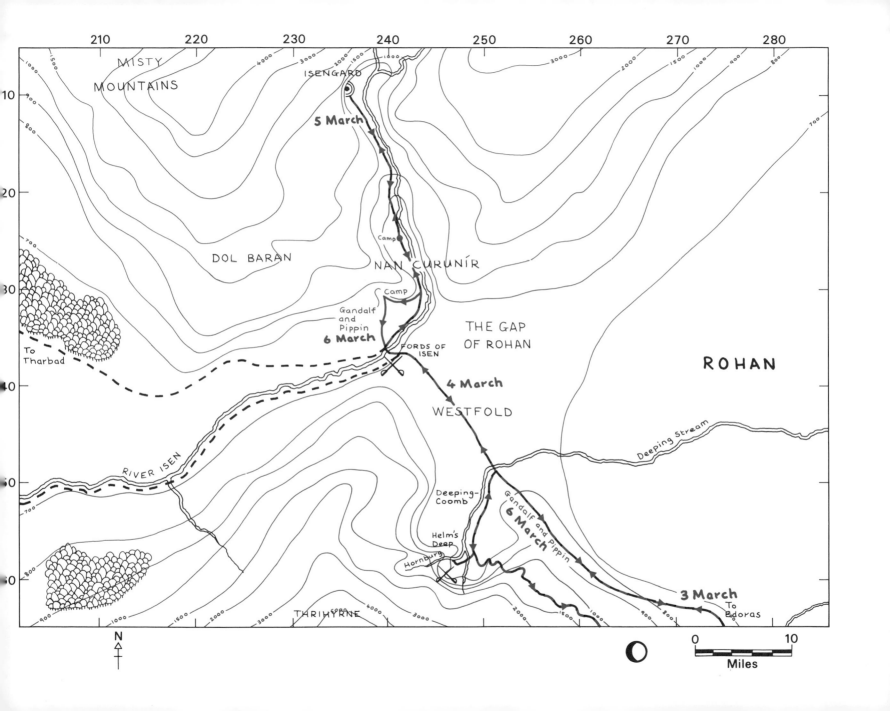

MISTY
MOUNTAINS

ISENGARD

5 March

DOL BARAN

Camp

NAN CURUNÍR

Camp

Gandalf
and
Pippin
6 March

FORDS OF
ISEN

THE GAP
OF ROHAN

ROHAN

To
Tharbad

4 March

WESTFOLD

Deeping Stream

RIVER ISEN

Deeping-
Coomb

Gandalf and Pippin
6 March

Helm's
Deep

Hornburg

3 March

To Edoras

THRIHYRNE

N

0   10

Miles

31. Helm's Deep

The Riders turned south along Deeping Stream some 15 miles short of the Fords of Isen.

I have followed Tolkien's picture of Helm's Deep. I have drawn the Hornburg in a loop of the stream, on a heel of rock sticking out from the northern cliff at the mouth of the deep ravine, where the Glittering Caves of Aglarond were. The Wall curved round the fortress and the road came in by a long ramp over the stream. Some quarter of a mile further out was the mile long dike and rampart. (Helm's Deep; Bk 2.) Death Down, where the fallen Orcs were buried, was a mile from the dike. (The Road to Isengard; Bk 2.)

The path shown leading south and up into the hills was the road taken by Théoden and his Riders, with Merry, (after leaving Isengard, Map 30) to summon the mountain men to the Muster of Rohan at Dunharrow. (The Passing of the Grey Company; The Muster of Rohan; Bk 3.) See Map 41.

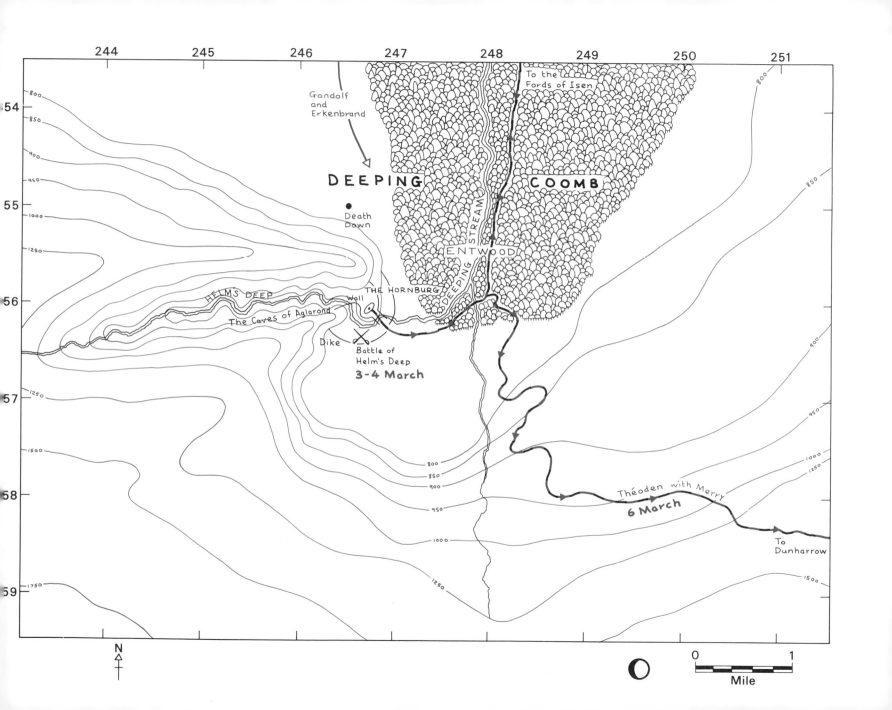

244 245 246 247 248 249 250 251

800
850
900
950
1000
1250
1500
1250
1500
1750

54

55

56

57

58

59

Gandalf
and
Erkenbrand

To the
Fords of Isen

DEEPING   COOMB

Death
Down

ENTWOOD

DEEPING STREAM

HELMS DEEP
THE HORNBURG
Wall
The Caves of Aglarond
Dike
Battle of
Helm's Deep
3-4 March

800
850
900
950
1000
1250

Théoden with Merry
6 March

To
Dunharrow

N

0   1
Mile

32. Isengard

There was only one entrance to the ring wall of stone round Orthanc. This was in the south. I have marked where the lake used to be, though it had presumably dried out by the time the travellers reached it. (The Road to Isengard; Bk 2.) The White Hand is off the map not far to the south.

Orthanc was made of four joined pillars of rock (there is a Tolkien drawing of it) and was 500 ft high.

When the Companions were reunited Gimli said that he had been chasing the Hobbits for 200 leagues (600 miles), but I think he was indulging in a little pardonable exaggeration, as I cannot make it more than about 500 miles. (The Road to Isengard; Bk 2.)

I have shown the gorge and the bridge where the Orcs crossed, and the main Ent dam of the Isen. (Flotsam and Jetsam; Bk 2.) Merry and Pippin came in from the north down the long ravine on the slopes of Mount Methedras. (See Map 28.)

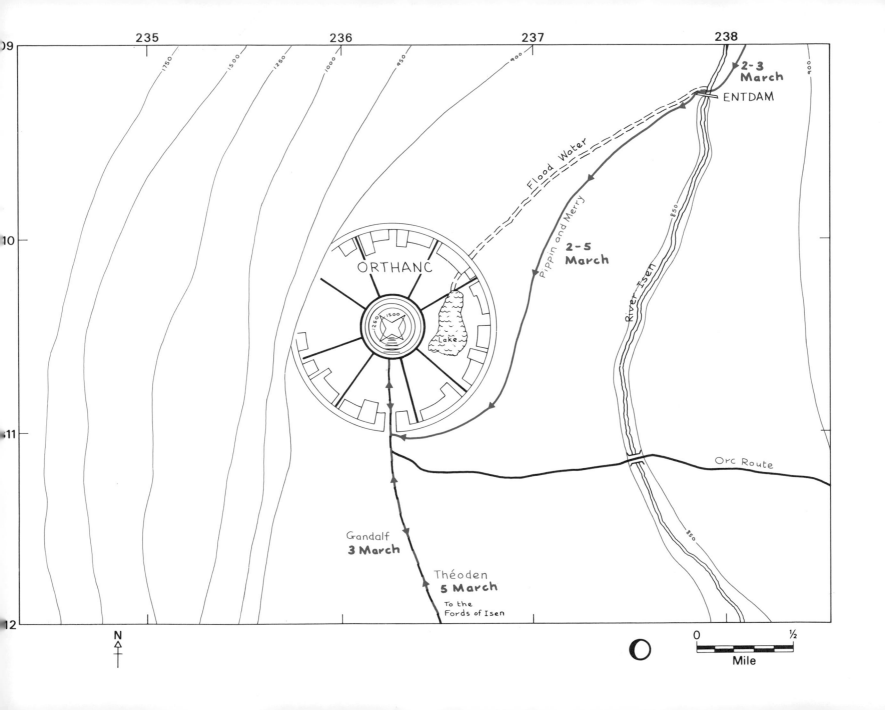

33. Fords of Isen to Minas Tirith

This map shows the whole course of the ride of Gandalf and Pippin on Shadowfax from the Fords of Isen to Minas Tirith, passing Helm's Deep, Edoras, and the seven great beacons, Halifirien, Calenhad, Min-Rimmon, Erelas, Nardol, Eilenach and Amon Dín. (See also Map 30.) The overall distance was around 440 miles; some 135 from the Fords to Edoras and 306 from Edoras to Minas Tirith. (Helm's Deep; Bk 2; The Muster of Rohan; Bk 3.) Gandalf and Pippin covered the whole of this in four days, whereas the Riders of Rohan took four days and a night to cover only the 306 miles from Edoras to Minas Tirith. But then Shadowfax was unique.

This map also shows the relationship between the point where the Entwash flows out of Fangorn and the junction of the Limlight and the Anduin, on roughly the same level. (The White Rider; Bk 2.)

As they started Gandalf told Pippin that it was 600 miles, as the Nazgûl flies, from Barad-dûr to Orthanc. (The Palantir; Bk 2.) If one adds together all the various distances mentioned between the two points this seems reasonable enough – 30 miles from Isengard to the Fords, 440 miles from the Fords to Minas Tirith (see above), 60 miles from Minas Tirith to the Ephel Dúath (Minas Tirith; Bk 3), perhaps 30 miles through the mountains to the Morgai ridge, 40 miles from the Morgai to Orodruin (The Land of Shadow; Bk 3) and, as I estimate, some 10 miles from Orodruin to Barad-dûr (see notes on Map 48), making a total of some 610 miles. I make it, however, around 100 miles less in a straight line. (See Frontispiece map.) Perhaps Nazgûls did not fly in a straight line. Anyway Gandalf had presumably never actually flown the whole distance himself and must have been guessing.

Gandalf and Pippin's arrival at Minas Tirith is charted on Map 39.

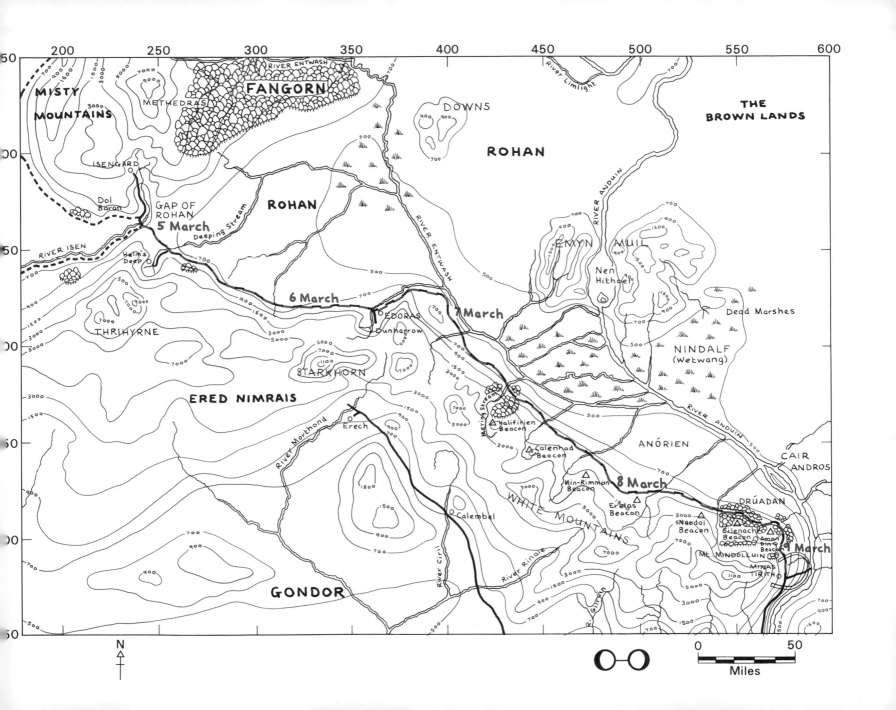

34. The Cliffs of Emyn Muil

This is a detailed map of the cliff in the eastern Emyn Muil down which Frodo and Sam climbed, and where they were joined by Gollum. It also shows the ravine down which Gollum guided them to the marshes.

This stretch is rather hard to follow, or at least I found it so, and I hope this map will help readers to envisage the route more clearly.

The route across the Emyn Muil is shown in the following map.

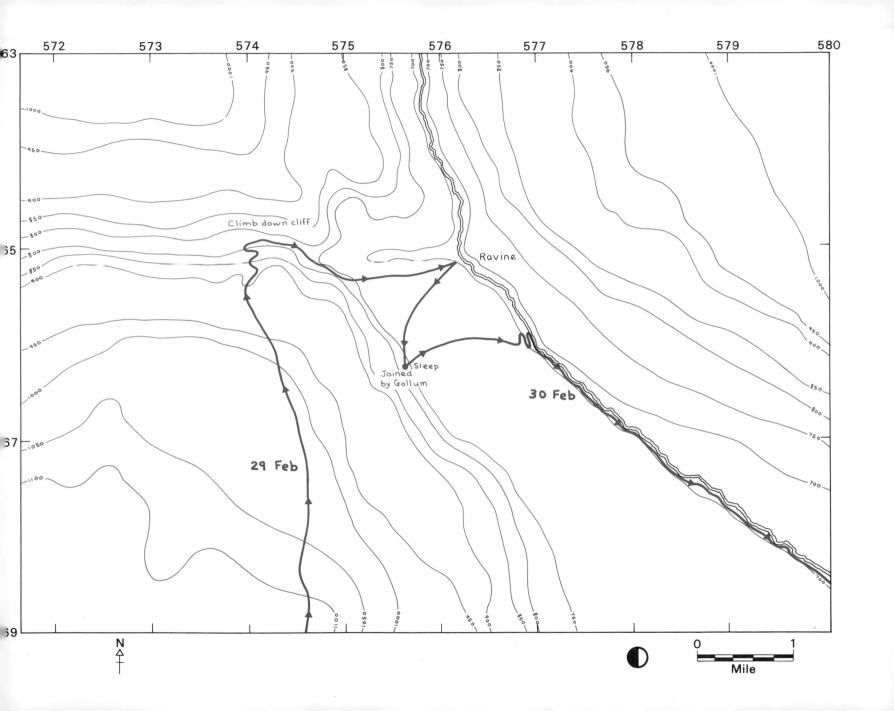

35. Emyn Muil and Nindalf

This map shows Frodo and Sam's route after they landed under Amon Lhaw from the lawn of Parth Galen. They made their way east along the southern cliffs of Emyn Muil, trying to find a way down, and were finally forced north until they were stopped by the precipice shown in the preceding map. (The Breaking of the Fellowship; Bk 1; The Taming of Sméagol; Bk 2.)

When Gollum had led them down the ravine he persuaded them to take his secret route through the marshes, and this was probably quicker (though more disagreeable) than going round to the north, although the marshes did not stretch very far that way. (The Passage of the Marshes; Bk 2.) I have shown the Mere in the Dead Marshes and also two streams running out of Emyn Muil further west, which are not specifically mentioned, to help account for the marsh.

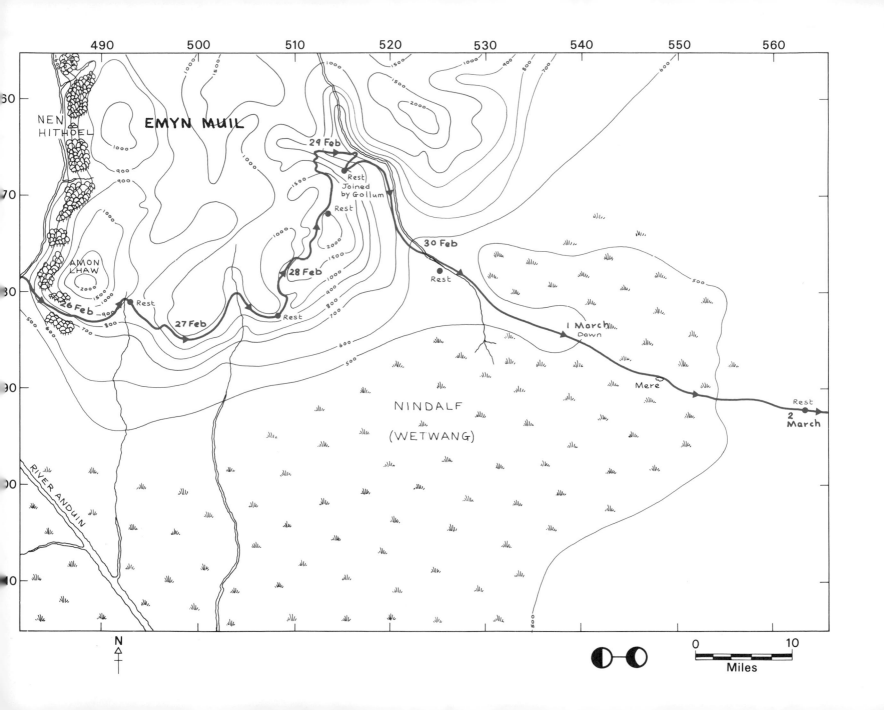

490 500 510 520 530 540 550 560

NEN HITHOEL

EMYN MUIL

29 Feb

Rest
Joined
by Gollum

Rest

30 Feb

28 Feb

AMON LHAW

Rest

26 Feb

Rest

27 Feb

Rest

1 March
Down

500

Mere

Rest

2 March

NINDALF

(WETWANG)

RIVER ANDUIN

N

0 10

Miles

36. The Gate of Mordor

One road went north from Morannon – presumably to Dol Guldur – and one east for fifty miles along the foothills of Ered Lithui to a point north of Barad-dûr. It had never been finished and stopped there. (Cirion and Eorl, Note 15; *Unfinished Tales*.) The third skirted the northern foothills of Ephel Dúath to the west and then ran straight south to the Crossroads in the vale of Morgulduin. (The Black Gate is Closed; Bk 2.)

During this part of the journey Frodo, Sam and Gollum travelled by night and slept by day. They rested on the low hill shown in the centre of the map and thence crept down into the trench-like valley between it and the foothills of the mountains, not taking to the road itself until they were round the corner and out of sight of Morannon. (The Black Gate is Closed; Of Herbs and Stewed Rabbit; Bk 2.)

The map also shows Durthang and the roads leading from it, one to the southern gate of the Udûn and the other south, past the Orc camps to the Pass of Cirith Ungol. (The Land of Shadow; Bk 3.)

Gollum said that it was 100 leagues (300 miles) from where they hid to the sea. I make it a little less south-west to the mouths of the Anduin, but somewhat more if travelling due south. Gollum admitted that he had never done the journey himself. (The Black Gate is Closed; Bk 2.)

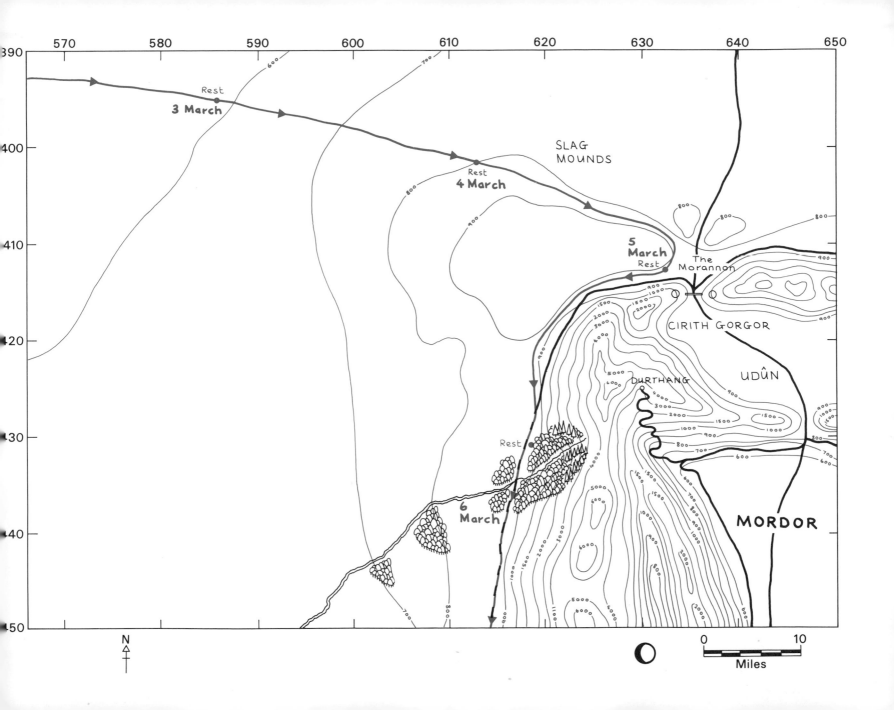

37. Ithilien and the Vale of Morgul

The trees growing along the slopes and bluffs of North Ithilien were mostly resinous: fir, cedar and cypress. (Of Herbs and Stewed Rabbit; Bk 2.) The travellers were now some 500 miles south of Hobbiton, about as far as Provence is from southern England, and the climate was distinctly warmer. The Vale of Anduin here was apparently more or less on two levels: the higher, which was heavily wooded and along which the road ran, and the lower fields by the river, which were less heavily wooded and very fertile, until devastated by Sauron. (The Council of Elrond; Bk 1; Of Herbs and Stewed Rabbit; Bk 2.)

It was about 100 miles from Morannon to the Crossroads. On their second day going south, after passing through a deep cutting, they turned right, off the road, and came to a small lake. Henneth Annûn, to which Faramir led them, was about 10 miles away and some 30 miles from the east bank of Anduin. It was also some 75 miles from Minas Tirith. (Of Herbs and Stewed Rabbit; The Window on the West; Bk 2; The Siege of Gondor; Bk 3.)

After leaving Henneth Annûn the Hobbits followed the sheer edge of the bluff south until the forest thinned out and they looked down into the Vale of Morgulduin. (Journey to the Crossroads; Bk 2.) Thence they turned back into the forest, then east to a hogsback and finally south to the Crossroads itself.

Going east up the Morgul valley they turned left just opposite the bridge to Minas Morgul, and climbed first the Straight Stair and then the Winding Stair up to the tunnel and Cirith Ungol. (The Stairs of Cirith Ungol; Bk 2.)

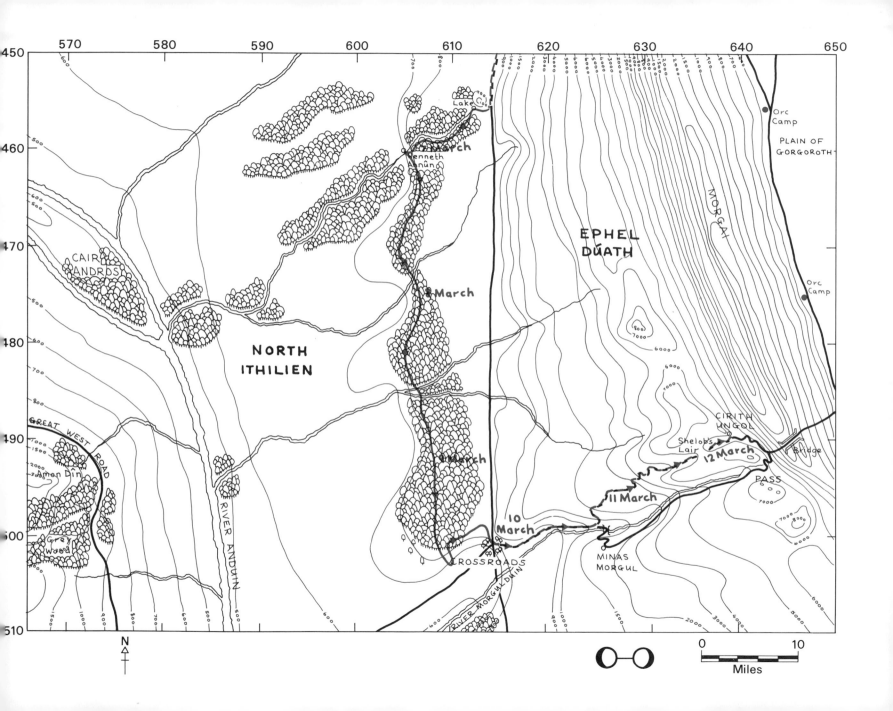

38. Shelob's Lair and Cirith Ungol

This detailed map is based on the Tolkien drawing of Cirith Ungol and the Pass.

The road in the main pass from Minas Morgul led up the south side of the river and finally wound left to meet the road from Cirith Ungol before descending to the bridge over the trough. Shelob's Lair was to the left of the tunnel through which Gollum led them, and there was also a side tunnel leading to the left, to the cellars of the fortress. The 'Horns' were peaks on either side of the path where it emerged from the tunnel.

I have probably made the bridge too long, but it was necessary to show clearly how it related to the trough between the Ephel Dúath and the Morgai ridge. (The Stairs of Cirith Ungol; The Choices of Master Samwise; Bk 2; The Land of Shadow; Bk 3.) The Dark Pass was higher than Orodruin, which was 4500 ft above the plain, which in turn I estimate to have been about 500 feet above sea level. The Passes must, therefore, have been over 5000 feet up.

The route continues on Map 47.

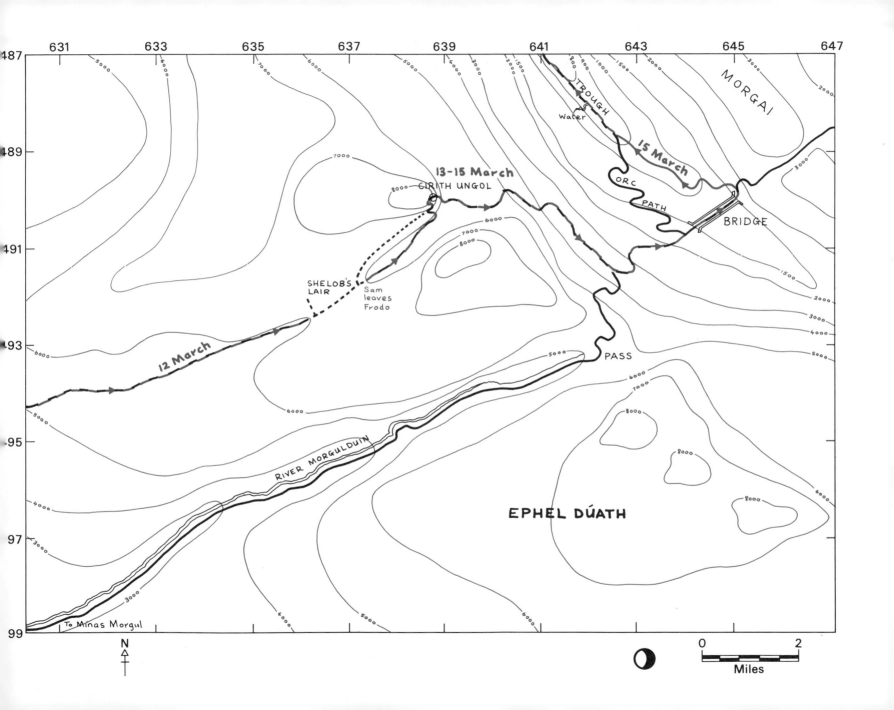

39. Pelennor

There were streams and homesteads within the wall of Rammas Echor. This ran from the mountains back to the mountains for 30 miles. At its furthest point, to the north-east, the wall was twelve miles from the City Gate, while at its shortest, to the south-east, it was little more than three miles. (Minas Tirith; Bk 3.)

There had once been bridges at Osgiliath, but these had all been destroyed, and now there were only boat bridges and fords. (The Council of Elrond; Bk 1; The Black Gate Opens; Bk 3.) The road from the city to Osgiliath led through a gate guarded by two towers and a walled causeway to the ruins. South-east of the City Gate were the quays and landings of Harlond. (Minas Tirith; Bk 3.) In my opinion these must have been outside the Rammas Echor. The Outwall rose from the very brink of the river along the south-east stretch where the quays lay 'beneath the wall'. (Minas Tirith; Bk 3.) It is arguable that the harbour lay within the wall but this seems improbable to me for strategic reasons, as it would have meant that there was a break in the defensive line of the wall.

The southern road from Pelargir wound sharply round the slopes of Mount Mindolluin and entered the Rammas Echor by a gate only a mile or two from the City itself – presumably the same gate that gave access to the port.

Gandalf and Pippin arrived on 9th March. The beginning of their ride is shown in Map 30 and the whole course of the route is detailed in Map 33.

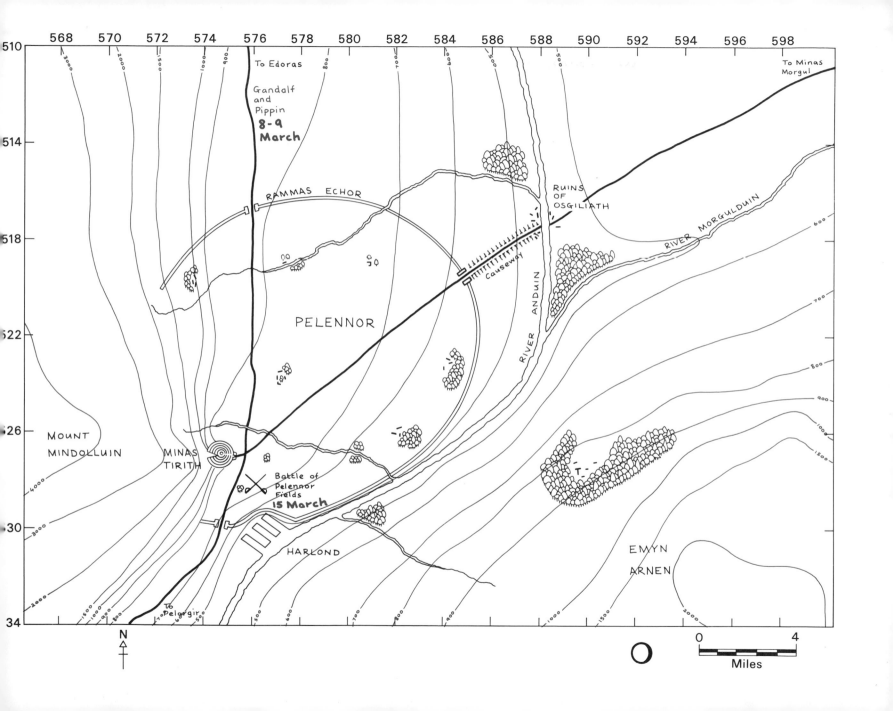

40. Minas Tirith

There is a very full and detailed description of the layout of Minas Tirith (Minas Tirith; Bk 3) which I have tried to follow. There is also a picture of the Citadel which shows the road running up out of the tunnel in the 'prow' and into the tunnel leading from the sixth level to the Citadel. This is shown as being a little north-east, as the 'prow' itself is due east.

The road swung across from north to south round the east side of the city, passing through the prow-like spur in a tunnel at each level. It must have joined the square in front of the Gate from the south.

The Tombs of the Kings were in the dip between the main mountain wall and the high spur on which the City itself was built and the path to it wound down from the fifth level. On the sixth level were the stables (Minas Tirith; Bk 3) and by the south wall of this level were the Houses of Healing. (The Pyre of Denethor; Bk 3.) The Old Guesthouse, which had two wings running back from the street, was in the Lampwrights' Street, on the lowest level, running straight to the City Gate.

The tower of the Citadel itself, which, following the picture of the Citadel, I have shown on the north side of the seventh circle, rose 700 ft above the City Gate.

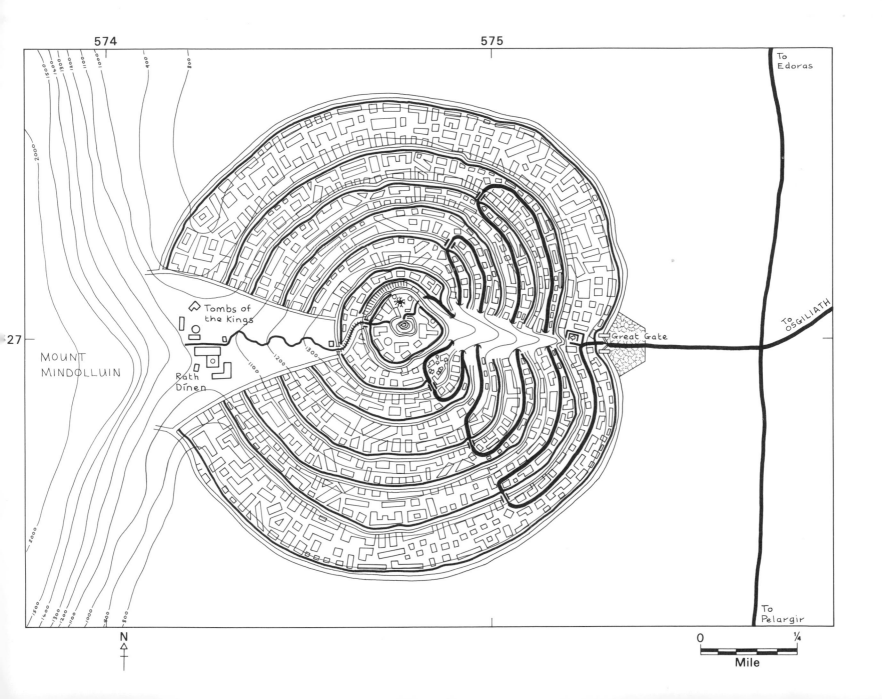

41. Dunharrow

The map of Dunharrow is based on the drawing by Tolkien as well as on the text. Harrowdale was about half a mile wide where the road from the hills to the west, the road to Dunharrow and the road to Edoras met. The Muster took place here, at a place where the Snowbourn ran close to the western hills.

Two villages are mentioned as lying between Edoras and Dunharrow: Underharrow and Upbourn. Only Underharrow appears on the map. (The Muster of Rohan; Bk 3.)

The Dwimorberg, beneath which Dunharrow and the Dimholt Gate were situated, was south of the mountain Irensaga and north of the Starkhorn. (The Muster of Rohan; Bk 3; see also Map 42.)

The road to the Hold on Firienfeld led up some hundreds of feet to a shelf in the eastern cliffs, winding steeply with a stone 'Pûkel-man' at each turn. At the top the road to the Dark Door was lined by standing stones. The camp was mostly to the right of the road and the Gate itself was hidden among dark trees, though they do not appear in the picture. (The Passing of the Grey Company; The Muster of Rohan; Bk 3.)

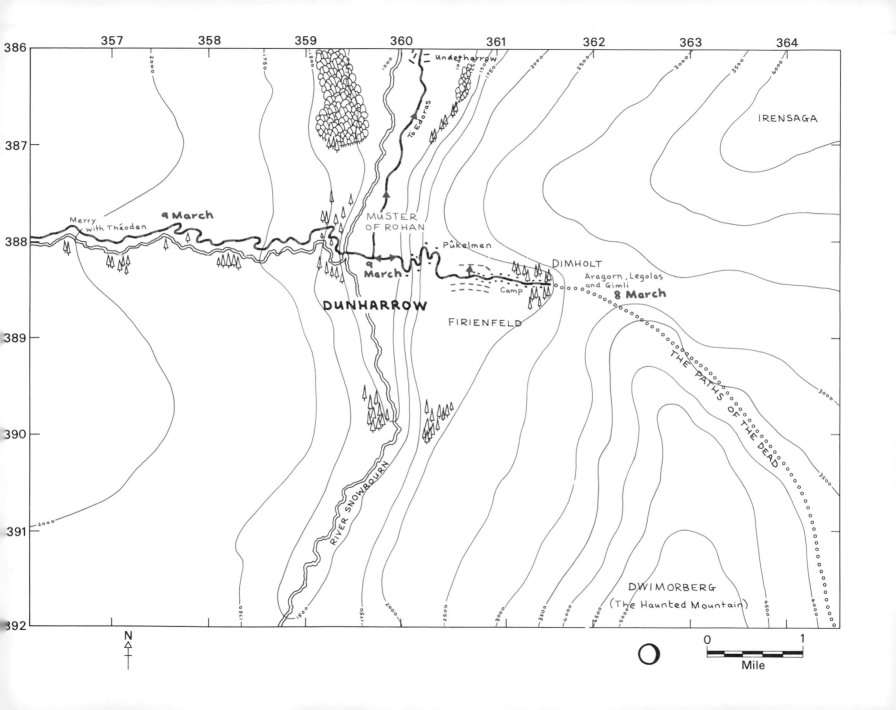

42. The Ride of the Rohirrim

The Ride of the Rohirrim started at Edoras and went down the Great West Road, along the same route followed less than a week earlier by Gandalf and Pippin. The first camp of the Riders was in the willow thickets where the Snowbourn joined the Entwash, 36 miles east of Edoras. (The Muster of Rohan; Bk 3.) They camped twice more, once probably in Firien Wood, and once more, possibly under Min-Rimmon, before reaching the bivouac in the pinewoods of Drúadan Forest. Mering Stream, which ran out of Firien Wood and down to the Entwash, was the eastern border of Rohan, and was fortified. (Cirion and Eorl; *Unfinished Tales.*)

Three of the beacons, Halifirien, Calenhad and Min-Rimmon, are shown on this map. Halifirien was the highest and was a sacred place, known as the Holy Mountain and the Hill of Awe. It was reached by a secret path through the wood and a rock stair. (Cirion and Eorl; *Unfinished Tales.*)

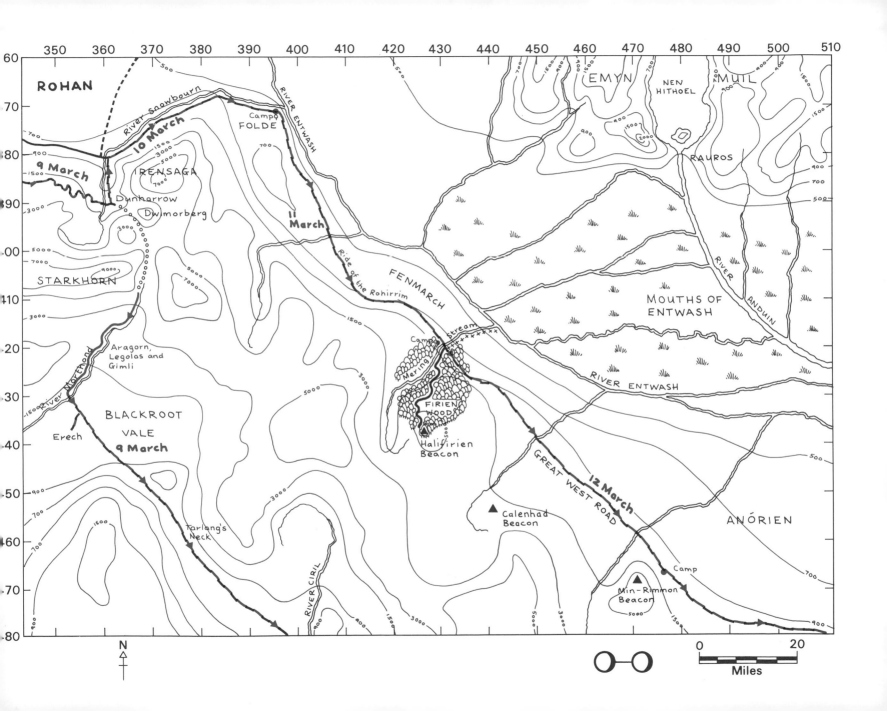

ROHAN

River Snowbourn

10 March

9 March

FOLDE

Camp

RIVER ENTWASH

IRENSAGA

Dunharrow

Dwimorberg

11 March

STARKHORN

Ride of the Rohirrim

FENMARCH

EMYN

NEN
HITHOEL

MUIL

RAUROS

MOUTHS OF
ENTWASH

RIVER
ANDUIN

Aragorn,
Legolas and
Gimli

BLACKROOT
VALE

River Morthond

Erech

9 March

Camp

Mering stream

Firien
Wood

Halifirien
Beacon

RIVER ENTWASH

ANÓRIEN

Calenhad
Beacon

GREAT WEST ROAD

12 March

Farlang's
Neck

RIVER CIRIL

Min-Rimmon
Beacon

Camp

N

0   20
Miles

43. Drúadan Forest

The four easterly beacons are shown on this map: Erelas, Nardol, Eilenach and Amon Dîn, from which the Citadel of Minas Tirith could be seen.

On the fourth night of the Ride, the Riders bivouacked among the pinewoods under Eilenach, and here they met the Woses. They were now less than a day's ride (which judging by their progress to date would have been between 60 and 70 miles) from Minas Tirith.

Stonewain Valley ran south of Eilenach, between thickly wooded ridges, joining the road again south of Amon Dîn. Orcs were camped 3 miles west of Amon Dîn and were pushing west along the road. When the Riders came out onto the road again they were some 21 miles from the Rammas Echor, the Wall of the Townland. (The Ride of the Rohirrim; Bk 3.)

The Forest of Drúadan and the Greywood, under Amon Dîn, were given to the people of Ghân-buri-Ghân in gratitude for their help against Sauron. (Many Partings; Bk 3.)

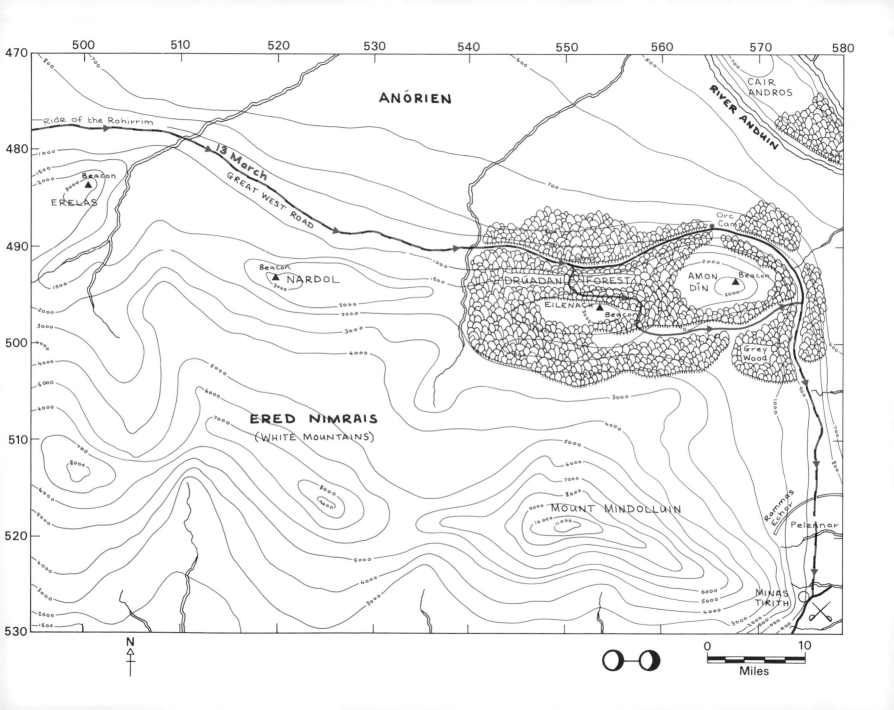

44. The Battle of Pelennor Fields

As King Théoden drew near to the Gate of the City he turned aside to attack the Southrons, and was sweeping them back when the Ringwraith flew down and settled on his horse, Snowmane. There the King was killed, and in his turn the Ringwraith fell, immune from attack by living man, but slain by a woman and a Hobbit.

The Rohirrim charged forward to avenge Théoden, and were supported by a great sally from the beleaguered City. The footmen drove south while the horsemen under Húrin, Hirluin and Prince Imrahil raced eastwards to support the Rohirrim who had been outnumbered and scattered by the Haradrim and their 'Mûmakil'.

Gothmog, the Ringwraith's successor, threw reinforcements from Osgiliath into the battle, Easterlings and Variags, and things were going badly until at the last moment Aragorn and his ships reached Harlond and attacked the enemy from the flank and rear. (The Battle of Pelennor Fields; Bk 3.)

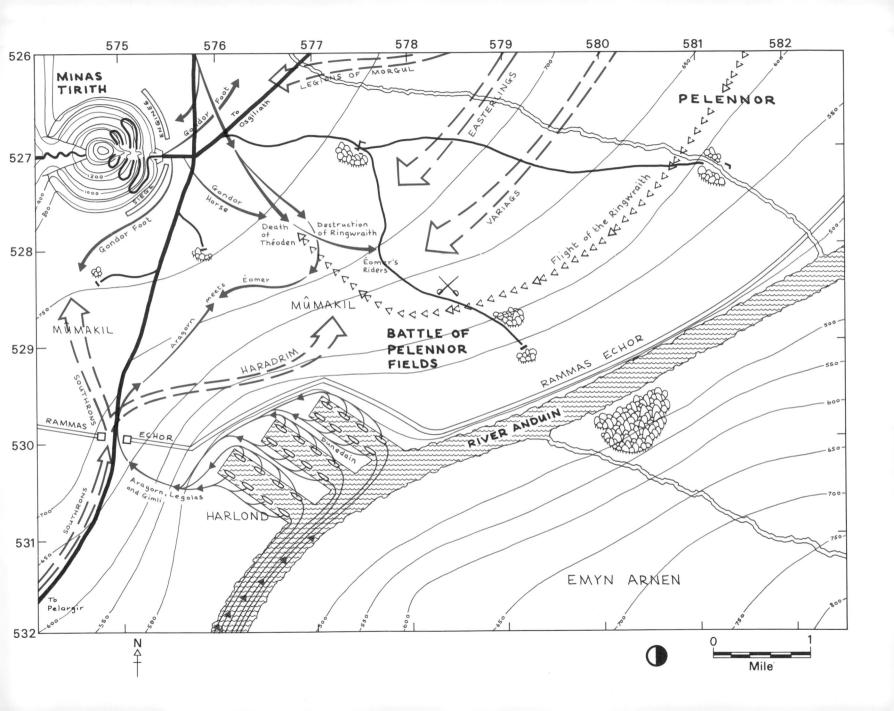

MINAS TIRITH

PELENNOR

ENGINES

SIEGE

1200

1000

800

600

LEGIONS OF MORGUL

EASTERLINGS

VARIAGS

To Osgiliath

Gondor Foot

Gondor Horse

Gondor Foot

Death of Théoden

Destruction of Ringwraith

Éomer's Riders

Flight of the Ringwraith

Aragorn meets Éomer

MÛMAKIL

MÛMAKIL

BATTLE OF PELENNOR FIELDS

HARADRIM

SOUTHRONS

RAMMAS   ECHOR

RAMMAS ECHOR

Dunedain

RIVER ANDUIN

Aragorn, Legolas and Gimli

HARLOND

SOUTHRONS

To Pelargir

EMYN ARNEN

N

Mile

0   1

45. Aragorn and the Grey Company

Aragorn passed through the Dark Door and into the caves under the Haunted Mountain before dawn on 8th March, and came out into a ravine, where the river Morthond ran beside the path, two hours before sunset (some ten hours). The distance was not great – probably not more than about 25 miles – but the Riders must have gone very slowly in the dark and with many delays and interruptions. When they emerged from the caves they were in the uplands of a great vale and still had a long way to go to Erech, but they could now travel faster and reached the Stone – perhaps another 40 miles – just before midnight. (The Passing of the Grey Company; Bk 3.)

From Erech to Pelargir was 93 leagues (279 miles). The road passed Tarlang's Neck into Lamedon. This may have been a ridge; there was certainly a ridge of hills stretching south-west from the main range at this point, according to the Map of Gondor in *The Return of the King*, but to my mind it seems more likely that the Neck was a long narrow gully among the hills through which the road ran. (The Passing of the Grey Company; Bk 3.)

From there they went on to Calembel, a township on the Ciril, and thence to Ethring where they crossed the Ringló, and on the third day to Linhir, which was above the mouth of the Gilrain. It must have been some way up the river, as Legolas never in fact actually saw the sea, though he heard the gulls crying. (The Last Debate; Bk 3.)

There was a battle there between the men of Lamedon and those of Umbar and Harad before the Riders arrived, but both contestants fled on seeing the Grey Company. After crossing the fords, Aragorn's followers chased their enemies for a night and a day before reaching Pelargir where there was another great battle.

From Pelargir up the river to Harlond was 42 leagues (126 miles). On the first half of the journey they had to row, until the wind changed (as King Ghân of the Woses had sensed in Drúadan Forest) and they were able to sail up the last stretch in time to take part in the Battle of Pelennor Fields. (The Last Debate; Bk 3.)

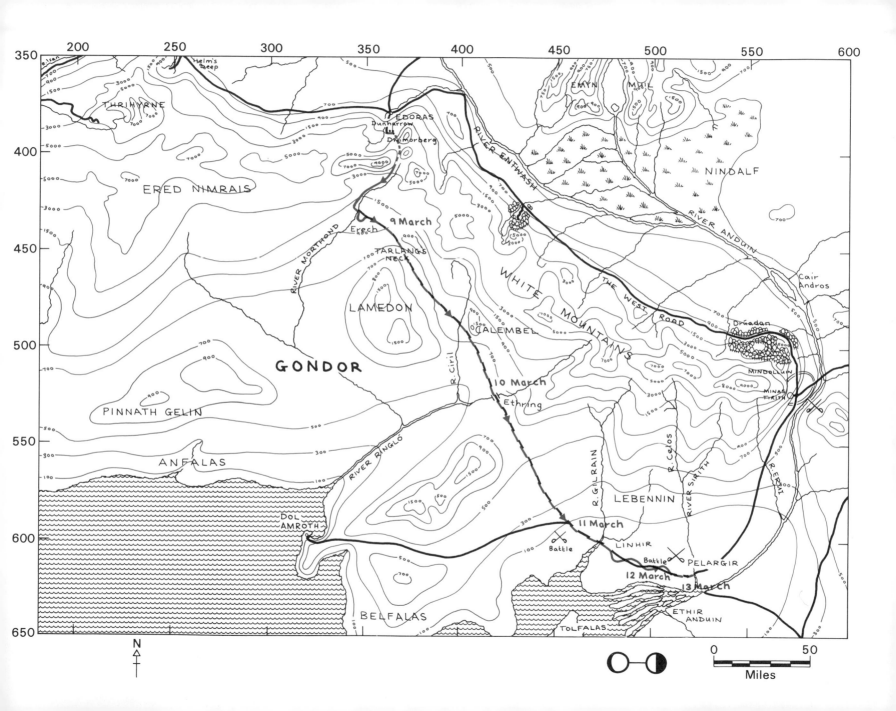

46. The Battle of Morannon

The Army of the West marched along the Causeway to Osgiliath and on for 5 miles to their first camp. The next day Gandalf and Aragorn rode as far as the bridge leading to Minas Morgul, which they destroyed. That night they camped close to the Crossroads. (The Black Gate Opens; Bk 3.)

They marched north and towards the end of the second day's march from the Crossroads they reached the cutting where Frodo and Sam had turned off the road and where the Battle with the Oliphaunt took place, and there fought off an ambush. On the fifth day after the Crossroads they made their last camp, after turning away from the road to approach Morannon from the north-west.

They drew up the army – now only 6000 strong – on two hills before the Black Gate. On one hill was Gandalf with the men of Minas Tirith, on the other the men of Rohan and those from the south. In the van were Aragorn and the Dúnedain, Prince Imrahil and the pick of the Tower Guard. (The Black Gate Opens; Bk 3.)

This map also shows the Field of Cormallen which was within earshot of the Falls at Henneth Annûn, and the route down to Cair Andros where the victors took ship and sailed down river to Osgiliath and so back to Minas Tirith. (The Field of Cormallen; Bk 3.)

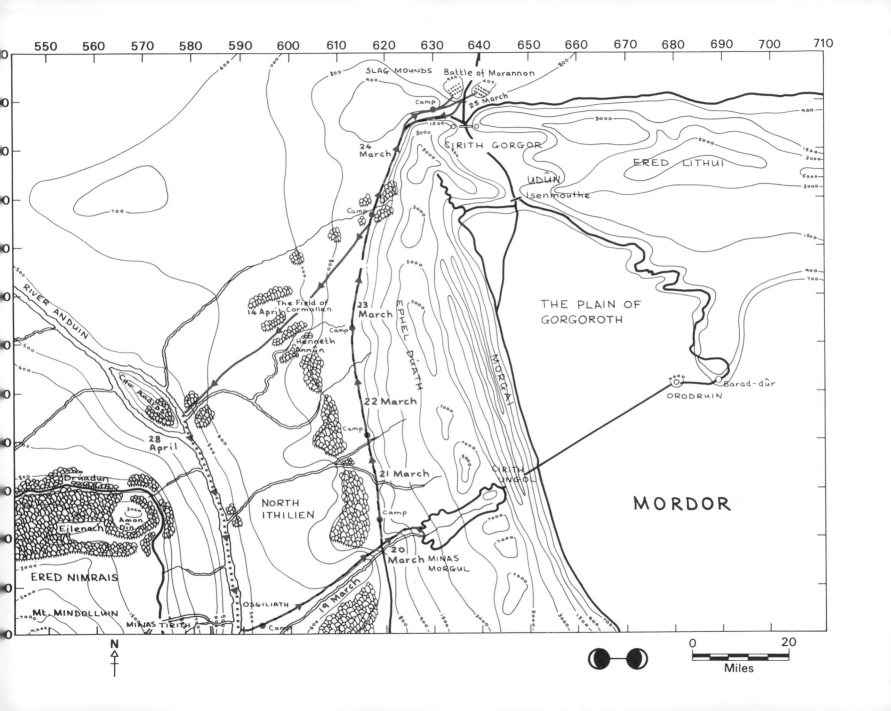

47. Gorgoroth and Mount Doom

The Hobbits scrambled down into the trough (see also Map 38) and soon found the Orc path which wound down from Cirith Ungol. (See also Map 38.) The trough was probably a bit higher than the plain, say some 750 feet above sea level. At the point where the Hobbits climbed to the top of the Morgai and looked east, they were 1500 feet above the plain (i.e. some 2000 feet above sea level, I reckon.) They were then 40 miles from Orodruin and immediately above one of the Orc camps. The distance from the bridge to the junction of the road past the Orc camp and the road to Durthang was about 60 miles, and from that junction to Orodruin it was also 60 miles.

At Isenmouthe, which was some 20 miles east of there, the Hobbits slipped off the road and passed along the trench and earthwall which joined the spurs of Ephel Dúath and Ered Lithui, about a furlong south of the road. From here the mountain appeared to be about 50 miles away.

Three roads met there, the western road to Durthang, along which the Hobbits had come, the centre road which led south to join the road running up the eastern side of the Morgai, and the eastern road which wound south-east to Barad-dûr. (The Land of Shadow; Mount Doom; Bk 3.)

The Hobbits followed this eastern road for four days until the mountain was almost due south of them, and, as I reckon, about 15 miles away. By this time they were not doing more than about 10 miles a day, and on the final stretch, going south, they were moving even more slowly and it took them two days to reach the foot of the Mountain. (Mount Doom; Bk 3.)

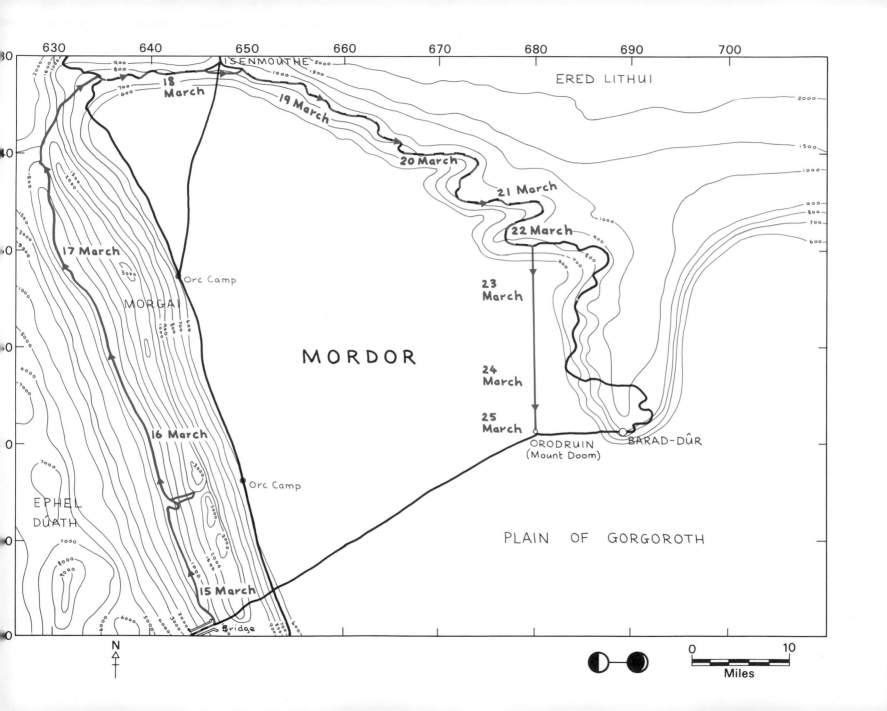

48. Orodruin

On the last day they struggled up the steep slopes. The base of the cone that topped the Mountain was some 3000 ft above the plain and the cone another 1500 ft up – as I make it, about 5000 ft above sea level in all. It was lower (though not necessarily much lower) than the Pass through the Ephel Dúath through which they had come. (Mount Doom; Bk 3.)

Judging by the Tolkien sketch of the Mountain the diameter of the base was about the same as the height above the plain, i.e. about a mile.

It is not stated exactly how far Orodruin was from Barad-dûr, though the pinnacles and iron crown of the fortress were visible from the gate of the Sammath Naur. It was a league between the western end of the bridge leading from the fortress to the point where the causeway started running up to the eastern side of the Mountain. It is unlikely that the whole distance was more than 10 miles.

The Hobbits climbed up the north-western side of the Mountain until they hit on the road which circled it. This led up to the Sammath Naur one way, and down to the Barad-dûr causeway the other, with a road branching off it to the south-west leading to the Orc camps in the south. They entered the dark cave of the Sammath Naur, reached the chasm and finally found their way down again to the point where they were rescued by Gandalf and the eagles. (Mount Doom; The Field of Cormallen; Bk 3.)

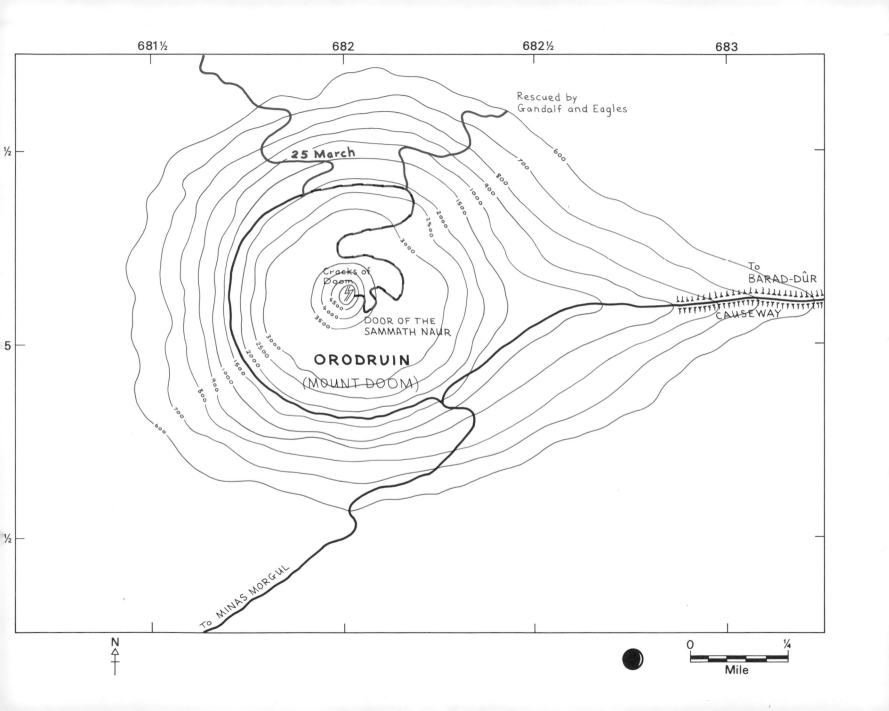

49. The Journey Home

The slow return from Minas Tirith to Edoras with Théoden's bier took 15 days. Thence they went to Helm's Deep and on to Isengard, where they said farewell to Treebeard and parted from Legolas and Gimli. After this they passed through the Gap of Rohan and made their way north on the west side of the Misty Mountains. After passing Dunland they came upon Saruman and at last came to the place where the road branched off to the Redhorn Pass and Moria Gate. Here they camped for a week before saying farewell to Celeborn and Galadriel.

They went on north again to Rivendell and finally turned west to Bree and *The Prancing Pony*, on to the point where they had left Tom Bombadil on the outward journey, where Gandalf left them, and so to Brandywine Bridge and the Shire. (Many Partings; Bk 3.)

There is conflicting evidence on the overall distance involved. In *Unfinished Tales* (The Disaster of the Gladden Fields, Note 6) it says that from Osgiliath to Bree, via Tharbad, was 392 leagues (1176 miles) and from Bree to Rivendell 116 leagues (348 miles). The latter distance presents no problem, but it seems to me that the distance from Osgiliath to Bree is improbably long. If it is about 20 miles from Osgiliath to Minas Tirith and some 440 miles from Minas Tirith to the Fords of Isen (see Note to Map 33) that would make it over 700 miles from Isen to Bree, and I cannot reconcile this with the many other measurements provided.

Incidentally Boromir claimed to have travelled 1200 miles from Minas Tirith to Rivendell (Farewell to Lórien; Bk 1) but it is not at all clear which route he took. He must have gone through Tharbad as he lost his horse there, so it is possible that he took the road the whole way. He may, however, have gone up the Hoarwell to the Last Bridge, though without a horse he would have found it difficult to carry enough food, while if he had gone up the Bruinen he would have had to cross the wild fenlands of Swanfleet and the river Glanduin. (History of Galadriel and Celeborn; Appendix D, *Unfinished Tales.*)

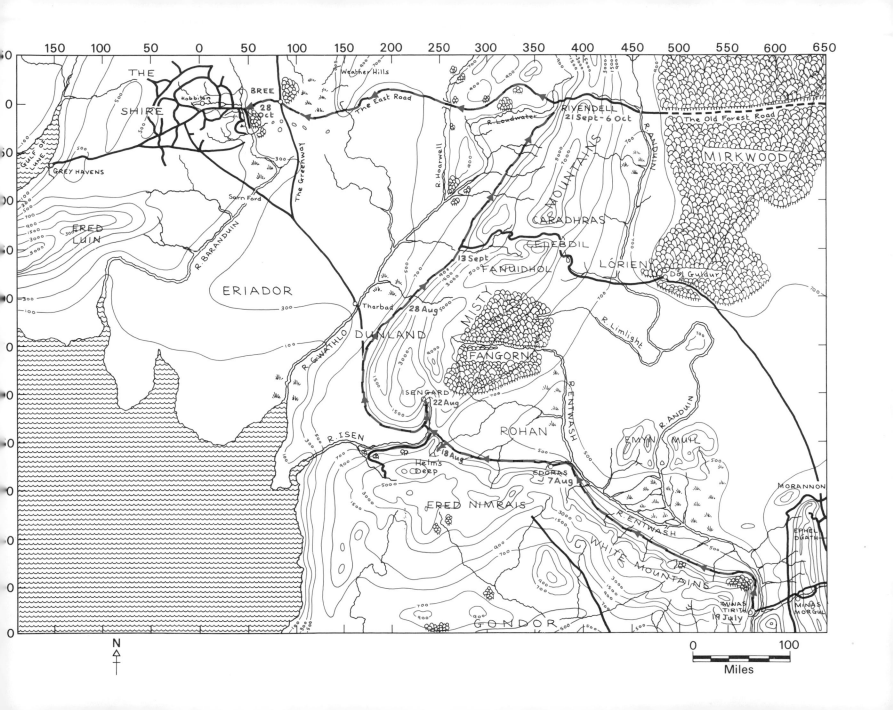

50. The Shire and The Grey Havens

Many details of places mentioned in The Scouring of the Shire can be seen in Map 2, including South Lane and Farmer Cotton's house, the Bywater inn and the avenue of trees which was cut down. Also Sandyman's Mill on the Water and the Old Grange on the side of the Hill.

There is a slight problem here. It is clearly stated in the Scouring of the Shire; Bk 3, that Frogmorton was 22 miles from the Bridge and the Three Farthing Stone just under 14 miles west of Frogmorton and 4 miles east of Bywater. But both the Scouring of the Shire and the Prologue to Book 1 say that the Stone was 'as near the centre of the Shire as no matter', while the Shire is said in the Prologue to have stretched 50 leagues (150 miles) from Brandywine to Westmarch and nearly 50 leagues from north to south.

My reckoning also makes the Shire some 150 miles from east to west, but this being so, the Stone can only have been central in a north–south direction, unless the Hobbits' 'No matter' was unusually elastic.

The last ride was leisurely – no doubt in view of Frodo's health. (The Grey Havens; Bk 3.) It took them 7 days after they joined Bilbo and the Elves, passing south of the White Downs and the Far Downs, across the Tower Hills and so to Mithlond, the Grey Havens on the Firth of Lune.

The mountains in the south-west corner of the map were part of the Ered Luin (the Blue Mountains). These also stretched north, beyond the river Lune, and there the Dwarves, including Thorin Oakenshield, still lived and worked in the days of *The Hobbit*. Gimli, too, was probably born there.

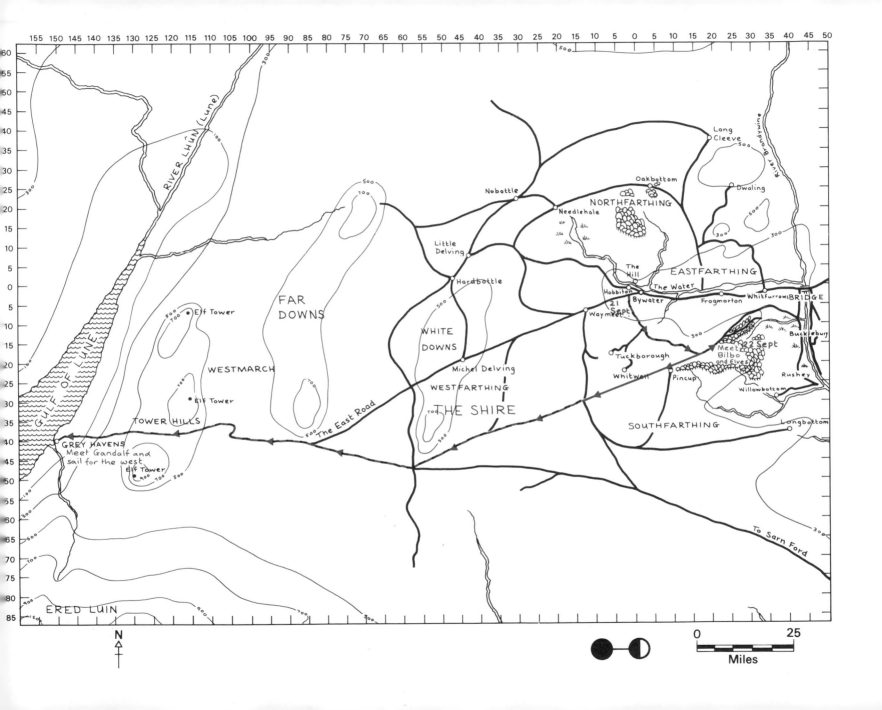

THE HOBBIT
J. R. R. Tolkien

The Hobbit is a tale of high adventure, undertaken by a company of dwarves, in search of dragon-guarded gold. A reluctant partner in this perilous quest is Bilbo Baggins, a comfort-loving, unambitious hobbit, who surprises even himself by his resourcefulness and skill as a burglar.

Encounters with trolls, goblins, dwarves, elves and giant spiders, conversations with the dragon, Smaug the Magnificent, and a rather unwilling presence at the Battle of the Five Armies are some of the adventures that befall Bilbo. But there are lighter moments as well: good fellowship, welcome meals, laughter and song.

Bilbo Baggins has taken his place among the ranks of the immortals of children's fiction. Written for Professor Tolkien's own children, *The Hobbit* met with instant critical acclaim when published. It is a complete and marvellous tale in itself, but it also forms a prelude to *The Lord of the Rings*.

'belongs to a very small class of books which have nothing in common save that each admits us to a world of its own'

Times Literary Supplement

'a marvellous fantasy adventure'

Daily Mail

'an exciting epic of travel, magical adventure, working up to a devastating climax'

The Observer

THE LORD OF THE RINGS
J. R. R. Tolkien

Part 1: The Fellowship of the Ring
Part 2: The Two Towers
Part 3: The Return of the King

The Lord of the Rings cannot be described in a few words. J. R. R. Tolkien's great work of imaginative fiction has been labelled both a heroic romance and a classic of science fiction. It is, however, impossible to convey to the new reader all of the book's qualities, and the range of its creation. By turns comic, homely, epic, monstrous and diabolic, the narrative moves through countless changes of scenes and character in an imaginary world which is totally convincing in its detail. Tolkien created a new mythology in an invented world which has proved timeless in its appeal.

'An extraordinary book. It deals with a stupendous theme. It leads us through a succession of strange and astonishing episodes, some of them magnificent, in a region where everything is invented, forest, moor, river, wilderness, town, and the races which inhabit them. As the story goes on the world of the Ring grows more vast and mysterious and crowded with curious figures, horrible, delightful or comic. The story itself is superb.'

The Observer

'Among the greatest works of imaginative fiction of the twentieth century.'

Sunday Telegraph

Three book paperback edition. Includes the full text, and complete Appendices and index in the final volume: *The Return of the King*.

One volume paperback edition. Includes full text, index and complete Appendices.

THE COMPLETE GUIDE TO MIDDLE-EARTH
Robert Foster

J. R. R. Tolkien's fantasy creations: *The Hobbit, The Lord of the Rings* and *The Silmarillion* have delighted millions of readers in recent years. Middle-earth, the world in which the stories take place, is as real and complex as our own. Events, geography and names were created with care and loving attention by Tolkien, who wanted every single detail of his books to fit into their total pattern. A belief in perfection, the fun of sub-creation and the desire to create something so totally convincing that the reader could believe in it (in a sense) as actual history, involved him in map-making, endless charts of dates and events and the development of his many invented languages.

The Complete Guide to Middle-earth is intended to add to the enjoyment of the reader of *The Hobbit, The Lord of the Rings* and *The Silmarillion* by bringing together in an A-Z sequence facts and information about names, languages, places and events from Tolkien's books which will provide an indispensable aid to every reader's discovery of Tolkien's world.

'a concordance to the names of people, places and things in the Middle-earth fantasies of J. R. R. Tolkien . . . page references are supplied to all British hardback and paperback editions.'

British Book News

'Middle-earth is the country of J. R. R. Tolkien's tales – the territory of Sauron, Bilbo Baggins, Gandalf and Sam Gamgee – whose legends, history, geography and inhabitants combine to make a unique fictional world. This Guide is a comprehensive reference work to every name and event in Tolkien's books, from *The Hobbit* to *The Silmarillion*.'

Daily Telegraph

Other books by J. R. R. Tolkien

THE SILMARILLION
The ancient drama to which the characters in *The Lord of the Rings* look back. It is the story of the First Age of Middle-earth.

'How, given little over half a century of work, did one man become the creative equivalent of a people'

The Guardian

UNFINISHED TALES
A collection of tales from the early days of Middle-earth to the War of the Ring.

'another monument to the incredible imagination of Tolkien'

The Sunday Telegraph

SIR GAWAIN AND THE GREEN KNIGHT, PEARL AND SIR ORFEO
Tolkien's translations of three Middle English poems. *Sir Gawain* is a romance, a fairy tale for adults.

Children's Books

FARMER GILES OF HAM
A tale of giants and dragons which no devotee of Hobbit epic can afford to miss

SMITH OF WOOTTON MAJOR
A folk tale and a short story *Leaf by Niggle*.

Books about Tolkien

J. R. R. TOLKIEN: A BIOGRAPHY
Humphrey Carpenter's acclaimed, authorised and illustrated biography of Tolkien draws upon private papers, diaries and manuscripts as well as interviews with family and friends. Now reissued.

THE INKLINGS
An engrossing story, by Humphrey Carpenter, of the Oxford circle that included J. R. R. Tolkien and C. S. Lewis.

Books by J. R. R. Tolkien in Unwin Paperbacks

The Hobbit	£1.75	☐
The Lord of the Rings one volume (*Unicorn*)	£6.95	☐
The Fellowship of the Ring	£2.50	☐
The Two Towers	£2.50	☐
The Return of the King	£2.50	☐
The Silmarillion (*Unicorn*)	£2.95	☐
Unfinished Tales (*Unicorn*)	£2.95	☐
Sir Gawain and the Green Knight	£1.95	☐
Farmer Giles of Ham	£1.50	☐
Smith of Wootton Major/Leaf by Niggle	£1.50	☐

Tolkien related

J. R. R. Tolkien: A Biography	£1.95	☐
The Inklings	£3.50	☐
The Complete Guide to Middle-earth	£2.95	☐

All these books are available at your local bookshop or newsagent, or can be ordered direct by post. Just tick the titles you want and fill in the form herewith.

Name ....

Address ....

....

....

Write to Unwin Cash Sales, PO Box 11, Falmouth, Cornwall TR10 9EN.

Please enclose remittance to the value of the cover price plus:

UK: 55p for the first book plus 22p for the second book, thereafter 14p for each additional book ordered to a maximum charge of £1.75.

BFPO and EIRE: 55p for the first book plus 22p for the second book and 14p for the next 7 books and thereafter 8p per book.

OVERSEAS: £1.00 for the first book plus 25p per copy for each additional book.

Unwin Paperbacks reserve the right to show new retail prices on covers, which may differ from those previously advertised in the text or elsewhere. Postage rates are also subject to revision.